THERE IS NO SHELTER FROM THE STORM

Sometimes the sky was white with bolts of lightning carrying unimaginable billions of volts of electricity. Sometimes it was as dark as the lightning paused to gather new strength. The noise was constant—the sound of the rain, the wind, the waves slamming against the shore, the thunder.

"I told you not to take all that stuff," a voice said.

"I didn't take anything."

"I told you not to take all that stuff."

He came into sight. Gwen looked at him. She'd never seen him before.

He wasn't the owner of the condo. He wasn't—but then she remembered who he was.

And that made no sense at all. No more sense than the knife he was holding. "But why—" she began.

"You know why."

He walked toward her. Gwen fainted away.

Also by Anne Wingate

Death by Deception

Published by
HarperPaperbacks

Anne Wingate

The Eye Of Anna

HarperPaperbacks

A Division of HarperCollinsPublishers

This is a work of fiction. The characters, incidents, and dialogues are products of the author's imagination and are not to be construed as real. Any resemblance to actual events or persons, living or dead, is entirely coincidental.

HarperPaperbacks   *A Division of* HarperCollins*Publishers*
10 East 53rd Street, New York, N.Y. 10022

This book is published by arrangement with Walker and Company.

Cover photo by Herman Estevez

First HarperPaperbacks printing: April 1991

Printed in the United States of America

HarperPaperbacks and colophon are trademarks of HarperCollins*Publishers*

10 9 8 7 6 5 4 3 2 1

For Alicia, who was three and living in Galveston County when Hurricane Alicia slammed in. She still remembers vividly her anger at hearing about all the things Alicia tore up. She burst into tears at a restaurant and screamed, "I did not!"

So this hurricane is Anna, not Alicia.

R ED AND GREEN MAKE BROWN.

But the liquid in the margarita glass wasn't brown, because blood is heavier than a frothy mixture of tequila and lime juice. The blood had run down to the bottom of the glass, and the alcohol floating on top had sealed off the air so that the blood hadn't darkened. Now it looked like some exotic red-and-green-layered cocktail. The tulip-shaped glass on the carpeted floor was almost the only small thing still upright in the entire room. Was that an accident—

Or—

Gwen put her hand over her mouth and ran for the bathroom. She vomited and screamed, and choked as the vomit and the scream bubbled out together. Then she bolted for the telephone.

Of course the line was dead.

She went down the stairs, stumbling in the darkness because the overhead lights were out. She heard glass crunching underfoot and knew why the lights were out, and she wondered why she hadn't noticed that coming in. But of course she had noticed. She just hadn't had any reason to care.

What if he's still out there?

She couldn't stay in the house, and she couldn't leave. Her car was a barely visible hulk in the distance twenty yards away. She had no idea where her car keys were—probably in her purse, which she had dropped somewhere in the house and wasn't about to go looking for.

The car was unlocked, because she'd planned to come right back out and bring in her suitcases. If she couldn't get away, at least maybe it would be harder for him to get at her, if she were in the car and the doors were locked—

Then she remembered the extra key hidden in a magnetic holder inside the front bumper. If it was still there, if it hadn't dropped out, if she could get it—

If she couldn't get it, and get back inside the car, and drive—

Start the car very carefully, very calmly, drive slowly, stay calm, stay calm—

If she couldn't get to the key, or if the key was gone, at least she could lean on the horn and maybe someone would hear her. Only of course nobody would hear the horn, just as no one had heard the screaming, because the pounding of the rain and the howling of the wind would drown out any other sound.

But you have to try. You have to try. You can't just sit and let somebody kill you.

Who was the other one? Judy was dead on the couch, her throat slashed. Blood had run down her arm, dripping into the glass on the floor. Josie was dead on the dining-room floor with a butcher knife in her back. *But who was the other one?* The one with silver-blond hair like Gwen's, the one dead in the bathtub with her face so cut and hacked no one could ever recognize her? What was she doing there? *Who was she?*

IT REALLY WASN'T GOING TO DO A LOT OF good to dry the clothes and then take them straight out into the pouring rain, but she couldn't wait for the rain to stop. It wasn't going to end anytime soon. Hurricane Anna's torrential rains and hundred-mile-an-hour winds were already so close that the afternoon sky was black and the palm fronds were whipping into shreds.

Katy's small frame house was only fourteen miles from Galveston Bay. They'd probably be stuck without power a week or more, just like last time. What this one would do to the yard and roof there was no guessing.

She had plenty of water stored, and candles, and tuna fish and things they could eat without cooking. But clothes! Ben and Danny had been promising for two weeks to fix the dryer, and Sears kept saying the parts were on back order. Maybe she could do without clean clothes for a few days, but the boys couldn't. She would have checked to see if Ben and Danny needed laundry done, but last time she'd done that Ben had rather stiffly reminded her they weren't married yet, and it wasn't right for her to be doing his wash.

Sometimes Ben could be so old-fashioned, even if he was a darling.

Anyway, Danny, at sixteen, was old enough that it wouldn't matter so much if he had to wear the same clothes several days in a row. Not like her boys, Steve and Joey, ten and eight, who were always filthy by evening.

Then she laughed at herself for worrying about Danny's laundry anyway. What on earth was she thinking of?

Katy stacked the second basket on top of the first so that she could carry them both at once, and leaned against the door to push it open with her hip. She almost fell when the door was abruptly opened from the outside.

"Oh, thanks," she said to her unseen helper, and hastily loaded the two baskets into the trunk without getting more than the top layer wet. Shaking the rain off her silver-blond hair as she returned for the third basket, she stumbled in the sudden darkness. Now why in the world had the lights been turned off? It was only four o'clock, and this was an all-night laundry, anyway.

Then she saw, reflecting the yellow of the streetlights, the dull gleam of the knife.

THE POWER WENT OFF ABRUPTLY IN THE MID-
dle of the news. "Damn," Mark Shigata said. "Well, I knew
that was coming. But I was hoping to get the weather."

As chief of police, he had access to all kinds of official
weather broadcasts, but they didn't tell him as much as he
could get from seeing the television broadcasts of the satel-
lite pictures. For nearly a week he'd been watching Anna
build, a malevolent spider of winds and rain drawing
strength from the waters beneath her. By now she was very
near Galveston, her far-flung legs already reaching inland.
But where was her heart? In what direction was she strid-
ing?

"The phone is out, too," Gail said. At thirteen, she took
a ghoulish satisfaction in being the bearer of bad news.

"I noticed," Shigata replied. "Now that you mention it."
He looked around at Melissa, who was on her way to
the kitchen. Her hair had lightened to silver-blond during
the summer, the result of all that time she'd spent on the
beach with Gail. Now, in the near darkness, Melissa's hair
gleamed eerily as she moved between the cabinet and the
stove.

"It's finished," she said tranquilly, as she began serving the supper Shigata didn't want and didn't know how to refuse. "I was going to put it on trays, so you wouldn't have to leave the news, but now . . ."

"We can eat in the kitchen," he agreed. "Gail, go help your mom."

Almost six months. Early March to late August. Almost six months she's slept in my house, in that tiny, chaste, third bedroom. Almost six months she's cooked my meals and sat across the table from me as I ate. Almost six months she's washed my clothes and mended them. Almost six months she's sat in a chair in my living room at night, reading quietly.

She watches television if I turn it on, but she never turns it on herself. She goes to the library when I'm not home and brings home books and reads them. She plants flowers and picks them and arranges them in vases. She never asks me for anything, and if I give her something she smiles a little, serene smile and says thank you like a polite little girl, and whatever it is, I never see it again.

I have never heard her laugh or cry. I have never heard her raise her voice since she shouted the day we met, when I shot her husband—my cousin, my double—and she shot me, thinking she was shooting her husband.

He had brutalized her all the years they were married. The first thing she said to me, after she understood I wasn't Sam, was, "You look so much like Sam."

She is the mother of my daughter, and I have never touched her. She is the woman I love, and I may never be allowed to touch her. How much longer can this go on before I go completely mad?

But I can't let Gail see my frustration. Gail is only thirteen. Thirteen is a difficult age to be, even for a child who didn't last year lose the woman she thought was her mother to murder, didn't see her natural father commit murder and think then that he was the adoptive father she loved and trusted, didn't discover a different mother she'd never known she had.

If Melissa leaves now it could break Gail, even more than living in this limbo is breaking me. I must keep silent. For Gail's sake. And for Melissa's sake, because she has borne too much, and whatever happens I must never hurt her.

Maybe even for my own sake. What would be worse, to go on living like this or to watch Melissa leave?

I don't know. God help me. I don't want to know.

"Is anything wrong?" Melissa asked.

"No. No, nothing's wrong." He began to eat.

She'd planned the meal carefully. She always did. The last book she'd read had been something about lowering your cholesterol. She had put the book down and looked at him gravely.

Mark Shigata was a good-looking man, and he was aware of that. He'd been an FBI agent for almost twenty years, and a police chief for a little over eight months. A long time, in two tough jobs that began only after he'd completed college and law school and had been admitted to the bar. But his face didn't show much sign of wear. He was in good physical condition, and his posture was perfect. He was graying a little at the temples, that was all. He didn't know how good-looking he'd be considered in Japan. He was a little stockier than most Japanese men he'd met, and his family had left Japan generations ago. He knew without vanity that when American women—especially Anglo women—looked at him, they usually looked at least twice, and maybe more times than that.

All of them except Melissa. She looked at him only to study him, realizing he was nearer fifty than forty, making some sort of assessment she didn't reveal by words or gesture. It must have had to do with cholesterol, because she'd quit giving him eggs for breakfast and started serving oat-bran muffins with every meal.

He had no complaint about the muffins. They were fine, if a little monotonous.

The complaints he did have he'd never make. Not unless they came out one day in an explosion of rage and resentment at what she was denying him, and he hoped he'd have the strength to keep that from happening. She was denying him her body, her love, her self. All these things belonged to her. She had every right to deny them to him.

He loved her anyway, and always would.

"Melissa, you've got to get out of here," he said suddenly. "You and Gail. You *cannot* wait any longer."

She looked at him.

"I told you that this morning, and you're still here," he continued. "You can't wait any longer, Melissa. It's not just you. It's Gail, too. Get in your car and get out of here. Last I heard, they said the eye's coming in just below Galveston Island, and then it's supposed to move up the coast toward Houston and New Orleans. I want you . . . you need to head straight inland."

"Kingsville? Alice?"

"That direction. West or southwest. The storm's heading east and northeast. But farther inland than Alice. I know you can't get far enough in to get out of the rain—you'd have to go practically to Arizona for that—but at least go far enough to be out of the wind. It's going to be hitting here at about a hundred and twenty miles an hour, and it'll be spawning tornadoes all over the place. It's not safe for the two of you."

"It's not safe for you, either."

"Melissa, I'm chief of police. I can't leave."

"I know that."

She did know that. Unlike his first wife—Melissa's sister Wendy, who'd always whined—Melissa understood. She never complained; she never asked why.

"I'd rather stay, too," she insisted. "I've been through hurricanes before."

"Not hurricanes that made a direct hit here."

"Alicia did."

"That's true. But you were in a better house then."

"Stronger, maybe," she said. "Not better. Believe me."

She had hated the house where she had lived with Sam, the beautiful half-million-dollar mansion he'd built, not for her, not for him, but for ostentation. After Sam had died in the driveway beside his silver-gray Mercedes, she walked out the door and never went back. Shigata had gone himself to pack her some clothes, and she'd quietly replaced them as quickly as possible, making it plain she'd rather wear skirts and slacks from Goodwill than the designer fashions Sam had bought to hang on her back as a blatant advertisement of his wealth. She'd asked Shigata to take care of selling her car and getting her a different one.

She wanted nothing at all from that marriage. She had kept the money—several million dollars of it—only because she couldn't figure out a way to get rid of it. And she was working at that, Shigata knew. Charitable appeals arrived at the house every day. Melissa read them attentively, wrote checks, put the checks in envelopes, and asked Shigata to mail them. He never asked why. He never asked how much. He just mailed them.

"I'll leave in a couple of hours," she said. "Are you sure you'll be all right?"

He shrugged. "No," he said. "But I'm sure I have to stay."

Gail had been watching them both. "Do I have to go?" she asked suddenly.

"Yes, you do," Shigata told her.

"I never saw a hurricane before."

"And you're not going to see this one," Shigata said.

"You've seen more of it now than you need to. Melissa, just throw some stuff in the car and go. I know you made up an emergency kit weeks ago. I got the tent out last night, in case you get stuck. I don't know if it'll do you any good, but if you get far enough west it might. Gail knows how to put it together. There are two gallon jugs of water here. Please go now. Can't you hear that wind? The roads are going to be unpassable in another two hours."

"You have to drive, anyway," Melissa replied.

"I do. You don't. I've got a four-wheel-drive Bronco."

"With a high profile to catch the wind." She stopped short, glancing at Gail. "I'm sorry."

"Right now, I have to go check on stuff at the station," he said, glad to change the subject. "Please be gone when I get back. Please don't make me worry about the two of you."

Melissa looked at him. He'd give ten years of his life to have some idea of what she was thinking when she looked at him like that, but most likely he'd never know.

"What about the dishes?" she asked.

"Never mind the dishes. When the power's back on I'll do them, if the house doesn't get blown down. If it does, well, we'll have to get new dishes, anyway."

Gail giggled at that.

"I'll use paper plates from now on out. Please, Melissa, be safe."

She stood up. "Gail, see what you can pack in five minutes."

Shigata also got up. He looked at them both, repeated "Be safe," and went out the door with an ache in his throat that wouldn't quit.

Bayport, Texas. Fourteen miles up the coast from Galveston Island. Population, about ten thousand residents and an indefinite number of tourists ranging from zero to more than ten thousand. Twenty police officers.

Windows were boarded up. Officially, the town—like Galveston Island and most of the rest of Galveston County—had been evacuated. The people who could leave had done so, except those who thought it would be a lark to watch a hurricane come in. But the poor black population of Galveston had spilled over into Bayport. Many people hadn't left because they couldn't afford to, not because they didn't want to.

In the station, Sergeant Al Quinn—Shigata's second-in-command as well as his closest friend—was preparing to go home. He'd been patrolling for twelve hours, encouraging people to board up, encouraging people to leave, helping control the heavy traffic produced by the stream of evacuees.

"Everything clear?" Shigata asked.

Quinn nodded. "No reports of anything. Everybody's too busy boarding up to get into mischief. I checked all the laundromats and all-night stuff—they're all locked and boarded. All the service stations are closed. A couple of 7-Elevens were open, but I figure they shut down when the power went out."

"Our emergency generator is okay?" That was a silly question; he could hear it humming, and lights were on in his office.

Quinn nodded. "Now I gotta go home and finish boarding up."

"Can't those boys of yours do it?"

"They've been busy trying to get Hoa's shrimp boat into as safe a place as they can manage."

"Try to get some rest, Al. It's going to be a hell of a long night."

"It's going to be a hell of a long week. I just hope we don't get looters."

"We'll get looters. And no, we aren't going to shoot them."

Quinn grinned. "No martial law?"

"No martial law. Sorry."

"We could go home," Gail suggested. "I know the way."

"I know the way, too, honey," Melissa said. "But we can't walk it."

"Why not? It can't be far."

"It's twelve miles."

"I bet I can walk twelve miles if I have to."

"So can I," Melissa agreed, "but not in a hurricane."

"Then what are we gonna do? Just stay in the car? Can't we change the tire?"

"I tried. The bolts are rusted on. We can't get them off."

It wouldn't do any good to change the tire if she could. She couldn't drive any farther. The roads were too deep in water now, and the wall clouds—the part of the hurricane surrounding the eye, where everything is the worst, where the winds might hit a hundred and fifty miles an hour and eight inches of rain might fall in an hour—hadn't arrived yet. She didn't know when it would hit; she hadn't paid enough attention to the forecasts. But in the half hour she'd spent under the service station canopy wrestling with the nuts holding the tire on, the winds had picked up sharply. She guessed they were blowing at a steady sixty now, and gusting worse than that.

"Then we could just call Daddy . . . ," Gail began. "Oh yeah. No phones."

"Right. No phones."

"But we could just put air in the tire."

"We can't."

"Why can't we? There's the little air hose thingy—"

"I know," Melissa said, "but the power's off. It takes electricity to make the air hose thingy work. Come on. Get your backpack."

"Get my *backpack?* But you said we can't walk home—"

"I know," Melissa said, "but we can't stay here, either."

"Why can't we? We could get the boards off the door and go inside, so why—"

"That's why," Melissa said grimly, as the sky lit up with a mass of lightning, followed within a second by an incredibly loud crash. "This is a service station. If lightning hit the gas pumps—"

"Then where are we *going?*" Gail wailed. "There's nothing else here."

She was almost right. But Melissa could see one possible shelter. *Now* she might get Gail to it, but if they waited five more minutes she probably couldn't, and they'd be forced to try to ride out the storm sitting in the car. She didn't want to think about their chances of surviving that.

"See that bridge?" Melissa asked, pointing to a freeway exit.

"Yeah, but—"

"That's where we're going. All right, hold my hand and run! As fast as you can!"

The crash woke Gwen. Not the crash of thunder, but the crash after the wind caught a metal lawn chair that should have been put away or tied down and wasn't, and drove it through the plate-glass window that should have been boarded up and wasn't, into the ornate gold-veined black-glass mirror that should have been taped and wasn't. The mirror shattered.

Sometimes the sky was white with bolts of lightning carrying unimaginable billions of volts of electricity. Sometimes it was dark as the lightning paused to gather new strength. The noise was constant—the sound of the rain, the wind, the waves slamming against the shore, the thunder.

"I told you not to take all that stuff," a voice said.

"I didn't take anything."

"I told you not to take all that stuff."

He came into sight. Gwen looked at him. She'd never seen him before.

He wasn't the owner of the condo. He wasn't—but then she remembered who he was.

And that made no sense at all. No more sense than the knife he was holding. "But why—," she began.

"You know why."

He walked toward her. Gwen fainted again.

HE WAS WEARING KHAKI PANTS, EXPENSIVE khaki. They were cuffed at the ankle and folded up once or twice. With them he wore a white T-shirt, plain white, no lettering or pictures on it. That was all, except for a gold watch.

The khaki pants ought to have been clean, with knife-edge creases, not dark with rain and spray and dirty with sand. The T-shirt ought to have been white, not smudged and splashed with blood. The watch ought not to have been full of sand and salt, no longer running.

He ought to have been strolling just at the edge of the surf, throwing sticks of driftwood for a dog to chase. Some kind of big, expensive, but not showy dog. Instead, he was standing on a wooden deck twenty feet above the beach, talking with a police chief who hadn't quite yet accused him of murder, but who was certainly getting ready to.

"You walked down there in the dark?" Shigata asked.

The man looked at the steep flight of wooden stairs that led down the cliffside to the waterfront. Like the deck, they were gray and weathered; they'd seen more hurricanes than this one.

"I guess I must've. I was down there." He didn't look at Shigata. Hands in his pockets, dripping with sweat from the sticky heat in the eye of the storm, he was looking at the water. Only the water.

"What do you mean, you were down there?" Shigata probed. He'd already had one answer to that. He wanted another one, and he was going to go on asking until he got an answer that made sense or until the man shut up and asked for his lawyer. Shigata had offered to call his lawyer. He'd said he didn't want one.

"Just, I was down there. I mean, I woke up and I was down there. I was drunk last night." He turned to face Shigata, one eyebrow raised. "I didn't have to say that, did I?"

"No," Shigata agreed.

"Everybody told you that."

Shigata let silence stand for an answer.

"Okay. I was drunk." The man turned again, abruptly, to gaze at the frothy sea. "I was drunk. I was passed out on the couch. At my own party."

"Do you always hold parties during hurricanes?" Shigata asked. The question wasn't entirely sarcastic. Some people do hold hurricane parties. More than a few such parties, all along the Gulf Coast, have resulted in multiple fatalities.

"No. But it was my anniversary and the party was already scheduled. I was damned if I was going to let a hurricane boss me around. That all right with you?"

Shigata shrugged.

"Not very many people came," he added. "I guess most of them had better sense. And then on top of that I passed out drunk at my own anniversary party. Ninth anniversary, if it makes any difference."

"Does it?"

"Not that I know of. Not to me, anyhow."

"Then it doesn't to me, either."

"Or to her, I guess, if you come to that."

"We have to come to that sometime," Shigata said. "Look, I'm trying to be patient, but you're answering everything except what I ask. You know what it looks like. You aren't stupid. You don't have to talk with me, but if you're going to, then let's make it worthwhile."

The man shrugged. "Sorry," he said, without sounding sorry.

"Let's take it from the top."

"Again." It wasn't a question.

"Again," Shigata agreed. "You were passed out on the couch. What time?"

"How should I know what time it was? Do you know what time it is when you pass out drunk?"

"You're telling the story," Shigata said. He didn't bother to point out that the chief of a twenty-man police department can't afford to pass out drunk, or even be drunk— ever. Neither, Shigata would have supposed, could a top neurosurgeon—but apparently he was wrong about that.

"So," the top neurosurgeon said, "I didn't know what time it was. Don't know."

"Your brother says it was about a quarter to twelve. That sound right?"

"I guess. As good as anything."

"Then what?"

"Then I woke up. It was dark. There was somebody in the house."

"Who? Jean?"

"Not Jean."

"How do you know it wasn't Jean?"

"She was dead."

"Did you know then she was dead?"

"Of course I didn't."

"Then how did you know it wasn't Jean? Or did you know then? That's a serious question, Dr. Weston. I'm not trying to play 'gotcha.' You've indicated you knew then it wasn't Jean, so how did you know?"

Weston gestured futilely, trying to spell out with his hands something that couldn't be spelled out. "It just wasn't. I mean, how do you know? You just know. It wasn't Jean. I don't know how I knew. I—" He paused.

"Just knew," Shigata supplied. Well, sometimes people *did* just know.

"Yeah. I just know. Knew. Whatever. I don't know. Maybe the footsteps didn't sound right."

"Did you know who it was?"

"Uh-uh."

"Was it somebody familiar?"

He shrugged again. "I don't know who it was. I already told you that. So how in the hell am I supposed to know whether it was somebody familiar?"

"Most people have a pretty fair idea whether footsteps sound familiar or not."

"Then I'm not most people," Weston shot back. "And I was drunk. I told you that."

"That's right. You told me that. All right. So you woke up and there was somebody in the house and it wasn't Jean. What did you do then?"

"I got up and reached for the light switch and nothing happened. Well, you know how often the lights go out around here, especially during storms, so we keep a flashlight in the drawer of the end table and I tried to get it."

"Tried to get it, or got it?"

"All right, I got it. But it was dark in the living room and I fell over something. I don't know what. Maybe the coffee table."

"You fell over something and you think it was the coffee table."

"Yeah. And then I turned on the flashlight and it didn't— I mean I tried to turn on the flashlight and it didn't come on."

"Then what?"

"Then I heard the person running."

"Running where?"

"On the stairs."

The stairs led from the living room up to a landing that functioned as a little hallway. Off the landing across from the staircase was a bathroom, and on each side of the bathroom, opening from the ends of the landing, was a large bedroom. There was a long storage closet leading from one bedroom to the other, across the front of the house over the staircase, so that each bedroom had a window alcove. Somebody familiar with the house could get from one bedroom to the other without going through the landing at all.

"Okay," Shigata said. "You heard somebody running on the stairs. Then what?"

"Then I tried to go up the stairs."

"You tried to go up the stairs."

"Okay, I *did* go up the stairs, but I fell somewhere at the top."

"Why did you fall?"

"What do you mean why did I fall? I was drunk and I was running up a steep staircase in the dark. Do I need any other reason to fall?"

"No, but you said—"

"Oh, yeah. About somebody hitting me. Somebody did, but not then."

"Okay, when?"

"Let me tell it, all right? I went up the stairs and I stumbled once. I guess I didn't exactly fall, you know, like falling down the stairs, I just sort of stumbled and barked my shin. Then I went into Teddy's bedroom—"

"Why Teddy's?" Shigata interrupted. "I thought you told me Teddy wasn't there."

"He wasn't. Look, Teddy's seven, okay? And we didn't want him there at a party where there was going to be drinking and so on. So he spent the night with the babysitter. But—look, you've got to understand how the house is laid out. Because it's funny."

"I've been in it."

"Yeah, but you may not have noticed, we had it enlarged. Remodeled. And we built this sort of upstairs back porch, like a deck, only roofed over. It goes across the whole back of the house. But the way the place is laid out, we couldn't put the door to it from our bedroom because then we wouldn't have had any place to put the bed except in the middle of the room, and we couldn't put the door to it through the bathroom, of course. So we put the door where you reach it going through Teddy's room. Of course we keep it locked all the time—a key lock—so Teddy can't get out unless we open it for him. But it turns out the lock isn't real good, or at least the door and the door frame aren't, and we've had kids break in the house a few times, just for larks, you know. They climb up the back fence by the garage and then climb from the back fence up to the deck."

"You haven't reported any of this?"

"I told you it was just kids. They never took anything. They only—" He stopped abruptly.

"They only what?"

"Never mind."

"What were you going to say?"

"Oh, hell."

Whatever it was, the doctor seemed far more upset about it than he seemed over the murder of his wife—although that thought probably wasn't fair, Shigata told himself. It wasn't very long ago that his own wife—his estranged wife—had been murdered. He'd been far more concerned, then, about clearing himself of the murder than he'd been about the murder itself. And there had been other things he'd been even more concerned about, like getting his missing daughter home safely. But Richard Weston didn't have a missing child.

"Whatever it is, you'd be better off telling me than leaving me to guess and maybe guess wrong," Shigata said.

"All right. It's not illegal. I mean, it's not like kiddie porn or something. That stuff turns my stomach. But I've got a sort of—call it a collection—of art movies, you know? On video?"

"I see," Shigata said. "So kids were breaking in when you and your wife weren't home to share the goodies, so to speak?"

"Yeah. One time they stole a hundred dollars out of my dresser drawer. But there wasn't any use reporting that. I never would have gotten it back, and I shouldn't have had it in my dresser drawer, anyway. I started locking up the videos in my gun case. They tried a time or two to find them, and then I guess they gave up. But when I heard whoever it was in the house, I guess I thought it was one of them. So I went into Teddy's room to catch them going out. Okay, well, the door up there was still locked, and nobody could have used it. And I was dizzy. I guess I was still drunk."

He paused, and Shigata looked uneasily out to sea. It was calm now, there was even some sunshine, but out there, not more than four miles away at the most, was the other half of this killer storm. He didn't want to break Weston's chain of thought by interrupting, but pretty soon they would have to get inside again.

When the wall clouds—literally a black wall of clouds, wind, and rain surrounding the eye—hit, they'd go in less than a minute from a near calm, with the sun shining and a gentle breeze playing, right into the worst weather this storm carried, with winds a hundred and fifty miles an hour and water like Niagara Falls. At that speed, a piece of straw became a projectile that could drive through a two-inch-thick wood plank like a bullet through Jell-O. The most secure house afforded about as much protection as a bamboo shack.

All this was what made Weston's story so very unlikely.

"So I lay down on Teddy's bed and I guess I—" Weston paused again.

"Went back to sleep?" Shigata asked delicately.

"Or passed out again. In retrospect, I guess he'd just stopped walking, and I couldn't hear him breathing because of the air conditioner—I guess you noticed we have room air conditioners instead of central air. But I didn't think of that then. Tell the truth, I don't think I thought anything then. I just lay down. That's all. Then—I don't know how much later it was—I woke up and heard somebody on the stairs again, and it still wasn't Jean. I went out and went down the stairs after the person—" He stopped. "It was dumb of me to check that door from Teddy's room to the deck, wasn't it?"

"Why was that dumb?" *What was dumb was telling me that the air conditioner was running. Unless you have your own generator—and if you do I haven't seen it—you haven't had electricity in two days.*

"Because I heard him going up the stairs. That means he had to be coming in from outside. So he couldn't have come in through Teddy's room if he came in an outside door downstairs."

"That makes sense," Shigata agreed.

"Okay, so anyway I went charging back down the stairs and then whoever it was tried to slug me with something. It whizzed past my face and caught my shoulder and I fell down the last two or three steps. Somebody jumped over me and ran out the back door, and I got up and went out after them, and—"

"Them?" Shigata interrupted. "You've said that several times."

"Him or her," Weston clarified. "I went after whoever it was and the wind promptly knocked me over. That's all I remember until I woke up down on the beach, half in the water. I think it was the tide coming in that woke me, but I wouldn't swear to it."

"Weston," Shigata interrupted, "the tide hasn't been *out* in days." When the storm had first entered the Gulf of Mexico, the water all along the coast rose to three or so feet above normal high tide, and there it would stay until the storm was over.

"Oh, yeah," Weston said. "Well, I don't know. All I know is I woke up on the beach partly in the water. For all I know, I might've fallen in the water and that was what woke me up. Anyway, then I went back up to the house. I didn't have any keys and I kept yelling at Jean—"

"Just a minute," Shigata said. "When you came out the back door, did you shut it?"

"I don't remember shutting it. But I might've, just sort of a reflex action or something."

"Is it on a spring lock?"

"What?"

"Does it lock automatically when you shut the door?"

"Oh. No, we have deadbolts. You have to lock them with a key. It's sort of a nuisance sometimes, but here on the beach—"

"So why did you need your key to get in if you didn't need your key to get out?"

"Because all the doors—Oh, I see—the doors were all locked. There are three outside doors on the ground floor, and they were all locked. I checked them all and then I yelled at Jean for a while."

"How'd you expect Jean to hear you, with all the windows boarded up and the storm blowing?"

Weston shrugged. "I don't know. Maybe I was still drunk. It doesn't make much sense, does it? Anyway, she didn't hear me. Obviously. So then I climbed up on the deck and went in Teddy's door."

"How'd you get it open?"

"The door frame is pitiful. I thought I already told you that. That's how those kids kept getting in."

"That's my problem, Dr. Weston," Shigata said. "How did the killer get out? If all the doors were deadbolted so they had to be opened with keys and all the windows were locked, how did the killer get out?"

"Maybe the windows weren't—"

"The windows were locked. We've checked. You let Sergeant Quinn in the front door, and he heard you opening the deadbolt while he was standing at the door. He checked the other doors and windows himself. All the doors were deadbolted. He found where the upstairs door was broken open, but you said you did it yourself. All the windows were locked, and most of them were also painted shut."

"I'd have been smarter and better off to lie and say the killer broke open the door, wouldn't I?" Weston asked. "Except I wouldn't have been yelling at Jean to open the door if there was already a door open. Or if I'd already known Jean was dead."

Weston looked at Shigata. His expression was that of a con man who'd just wiggled out of a tight place.

"Telling the truth is always smarter."

Shigata didn't tell him that a next-door neighbor, hearing Weston yelling in the yard despite the winds that were by then about seventy miles an hour, had gone outside to see if he was injured, only to see him climbing up to the deck—rather athletically for a man who was supposed to have an injured shoulder—and hear him breaking the upstairs back door in. The door that should have been boarded up, but wasn't.

Shigata also didn't tell him that Sergeant Quinn had already found the keys Weston undoubtedly was shortly going to report missing. The keys had been in the sand beside the spot where Weston had reported he woke up.

"Then what?" Shigata asked.

"Then I went in the house and found Jean. I—I tried to see if, you know, if there was anything I could do to help her, but obviously there wasn't."

It would have been obvious to anybody. It should have been obvious from across the room, to an experienced neurosurgeon, that a woman in early rigor mortis, with her head bludgeoned and part of her brain on her pillow and part stuck to the wall, was beyond help.

Which made Weston's explanation that he'd gotten blood on the knee of his pants and on his right shoulder leaning over to try to help her sound a little strange. Especially in view of the fact that the blood on his shoulder was definitely a spatter.

And if he'd gone out in the storm at all, that spatter should have washed out. That suggested he hadn't gone out at all, not until the rain stopped, and then that he'd gone out only long enough to drop the keys Quinn had found.

But that didn't make sense, either. That neighbor *saw* him outside during the rain. So why hadn't the blood spatter washed off?

"Then I called my brother, and he said he'd call the police. I got my other keys and went outside until your Sergeant Quinn showed up. My brother got here about five minutes after that."

"Why'd you call your brother instead of the police?" Shigata asked. Shigata's home phone was out, but some of the areas with buried cables did still have service.

Weston shrugged.

"You remember the first thing your brother said when he showed up?" Shigata asked.

Weston shook his head.

"Quinn does. He told me about it. Your brother said, 'Richard, did you do this?' Why do you suppose he said that?"

"I don't know why he said that."

That was a patent lie. If Shigata pointed the lie out, Weston would bluster and deny it, and the lie would get deeper. But if Shigata waited, eventually Weston would get so nervous, on account of the silence, that he'd say something.

Anything.

No matter how incriminating it was.

Theoretically.

Which didn't necessarily mean the theory would work out in real life. Theories often don't.

But this time it did. Weston stirred uneasily, put one foot up on the railing of the deck, fidgeted a minute or two, and said, "We've been fighting a lot."

"Why?"

Weston shook his head and laughed uneasily. "You know what an open marriage is?"

"Suppose you explain it."

"Well, it just means I wasn't supposed to get mad if Jean, you know, went out with some other guy if I was busy and couldn't go with her somewhere, and Jean wasn't supposed to get mad if I—you know.''

"So you had an open marriage."

"Yeah. Only it sort of wasn't working."

"As a marriage or as an open marriage?"

"As either one. We'd been sort of talking divorce, only we hadn't come to any kind of agreement. Then Jean found out she was pregnant, and we sort of changed our minds and decided to give it another try."

"Sort of?" Shigata couldn't help asking.

Weston again laughed nervously. "All right, I know it sounds stupid. We had agreed to give it another try. That's why we had the anniversary party. It was a sort—I mean it was a second-chance party."

"At which you got drunk."

"At which I got drunk. Which might give you some sort of idea as to how well this reconciliation was working."

"A little indication, anyway."

"Listen," Weston said, "a divorce is cheaper than a murder rap. Especially in Texas."

That was true, in view of the fact that Texas law does not provide for alimony. But how badly would a division of property hurt Richard Weston? And how angry was he by the time the party broke up?

"Weston," Shigata said, "do you know what a storm surge is?"

"Should I?"

"I thought living in hurricane alley you might."

"Well I don't."

"It's a moving wall of water, a big pile of water. The storm makes it. It piles up on the northeast side of the storm."

"So?"

"So the storm surge came ashore about dawn."

"So?" Weston said again, sounding a little annoyed.

"If you'd been asleep or passed out on the beach at dawn, you'd either have woke up or died. That's all. But you didn't call the police station or your brother until nearly noon, after the eye came ashore."

"Maybe I landed on the beach after the storm surge. I know I spent some time inside before I called anybody."

"Doing what?"

Weston shrugged. "Checking on Jean. Crying. Walking around. I guess I probably was a little bit in shock."

"Is that a professional opinion?"

"Huh?"

"You're a doctor. Is that a professional opinion, that you were a little bit in shock?"

"Yeah. In retrospect, yeah, I was in shock."

"Are you in shock now?"

"No."

"Now I'll give you a professional opinion," Shigata said. "My professional opinion is you're lying to me. After the storm surge, the water stayed up. I mean, *look* at it! It should be pretty near low tide right now, but instead it's about eight feet *above* normal high tide."

"I'm *not* lying," Weston insisted. "I know I was down there. It was dark as the hubs of hell and blowing like a wind tunnel, and I figured I better get inside while I still could and worry later about how I'd gotten outside. I don't know what time it was. My watch is full of water, and you know as well as I do you can't tell day from night in a hurricane."

That was true. In the midst of a hurricane, day and night aren't much different. But Shigata hadn't believed Weston's story the first time he heard it, and every time he heard it he found it more implausible.

The black wall of clouds was so close now he could see its curvature. "I think we better go inside," Shigata said.

* * *

"Joey, stop crying," Steve begged, trying not to cry himself.

"I want Mommy!"

"Mommy'll come back, I promise. She always does, doesn't she?"

"I want Mommy now! It's been all night . . ."

"It's because of the storm. She'll be back."

"Why can't we leave?" Gail asked. "The storm's over now. We could walk home." She was trudging along, carrying things from the car, too tired even to splash in the puddles.

"The storm's not over, honey," Melissa explained. "Anyway, we can't get onto the road. We can get to the bridge or the service station, and that's all."

"The storm's not over? But the sun's out, and the wind stopped."

"We're in the eye of the storm. The storm is shaped kind of like a doughnut. The wind and rain is the doughnut and the middle, where there's no doughnut, is calm. We're in the middle now. But the other side is coming."

"You mean the wind'll be back?" Gail scrambled up the embankment with the jug of drinking water, put it down, and reached for the tent Melissa held up to her.

"Yes. The wind will be back."

"How much longer?"

"We've got time to get the rest of the things from the car. So come down now and—"

"No," Gail said, scrambling back down without the aid of Melissa's outstretched hands. "I mean, how much longer will the storm last?"

"I don't know," Melissa said. "If the eye comes all the way ashore it'll die down pretty fast, just a few more hours. But if the eye stays right on the coast, where it's partly in the water, then—Gail, look out!" She caught the child's arm and pulled her back.

"What's wrong?" Gail demanded. "I was just going to get on the road."

"Gail, that's not a road right now, it's a river. It's ten feet deep and it's got a strong current. You'd be swept away in a second."

"I don't like sleeping under a bridge." There was a distinct whine in Gail's voice.

"I don't, either, but we're safe from the storm there."

"We'd be safe from the storm if we broke a window and got in the service station."

"The windows are all boarded up. And we wouldn't be safe. I don't know what would happen if lightning struck near a gas pump, but I know I don't want to find out."

"What if a snake got under the bridge with us?"

"I'd shoot it," Melissa said, with more bravado than she felt. "Remember your dad gave me that pistol and taught me how to shoot it? I brought it along."

"Mom, if the road is flooded, then nobody can get off the freeway."

"That's right."

"And nobody can drive on the road from town."

"That's right, too."

"So there's nobody here but us. Nobody but us can get here till the storm goes away. We're all alone."

"Yes. But that means nobody can bother us."

"Mom, I'm scared." The whine was still in her voice.

"So am I," Melissa said. "But we're safe. If we can't get out then nobody can get at us, and the bridge will keep the storm from getting at us very much."

"What if the bridge falls down?"

"It won't." Melissa slammed the trunk lid. *Three days' worth of Kool-Aid, crackers, Vienna sausage, and canned beans.*

We've already been here almost a day. We'll be hungry before this thing is over.

"Are you really my mom?"

"I really am."

"Then why did my other mom say she was my mom?"

Melissa hesitated, and then decided to tell the truth. "Because your real dad was very bad. You had a half sister named Lucie, and he killed her. I was scared he'd hurt you. So I paid Wendy to take care of you and say she was your mom."

"And she was your sister."

"Sort of."

"She didn't take very good care of me."

"I know that now," Melissa said, "but I didn't know what else to do."

Something suddenly caught Gail's attention. "What's that?"

"What's what?"

"That flash. Over there. I saw something flash over there."

"Probably the sun on the water," Melissa said, watching clouds flood in from the direction of the sea. The calm wouldn't last much longer. "Let's sit in the sun while we can."

"It wasn't the sun on the water," Gail said. "I know what the sun on the water looks like. It was something else."

"Then I don't know what it was."

The binoculars caught the sun as he put them down.

Another blond. Look at the way she tosses her hair. Pretty as hell and knows it.

He let them kill her for a blond.

Not just any blond. It was that color of hair, that whitey blond. That might be the right one he'd left locked up, but then it might not. It might be this one. She had the shape for it—those tight jeans she was wearing didn't make any secret of that.

He raised the binoculars again.

"Why don't you marry my dad?"

"He hasn't asked me," Melissa said. That was the truth as far as it went. The rest of the truth was, he never would ask her until she indicated she wanted to be asked. "I think we better get back under the bridge."

"Why?"

"Because your nose is getting pink and I'll bet mine is, too." She tweaked Gail's nose and Gail giggled and wrinkled her nose like a rabbit.

That isn't the real reason. The storm is coming back. I can see the wall clouds moving in from the Gulf, coming so fast I can see the motion.

You cried all night last night, too, off and on, in your sleep, while the wind screamed louder than a train. In that loudness there was a special kind of privacy. I could hear the storm and nothing else, and that was fine, because I wanted to think about your dad. I wanted to think about Mark. He always looks at me, and looks at me.

He knows what I've been, what I've done. He wouldn't want to marry me. Maybe he thinks he would, but he'll get over that—and that's fine, because if he married me he'd expect me to sleep with him and I don't want to. I hate that. I always have.

I know when he wants to do that because he looks at me. He doesn't look furtively, but he doesn't look long. He looks away. He looks sad.

Most men would just do it if they wanted to, but he doesn't. I asked him one time why he didn't and he said, "Melissa, how many times have you been raped?" I didn't answer because I really couldn't remember and he said, "I won't rape you." I told him he wouldn't have to because I'd let him, and he looked at me and

said, "You've never not been raped. You don't even know the difference."

*I think he would try not to hurt me. I think he would try to
make me like it. I wish I could like it, the way other people do.*

Mark Shigata is the only clean man I have ever met.

*I don't want to sleep with him because I don't want to sleep with
anybody, but I think I'll die if he ever makes me leave.*

"Mom? Are you all right?"

"Oh, yes. Just sleepy." She wriggled around on the tent
canvas, trying to get comfortable, but that was a lost cause.
Besides that, her breasts felt full and heavy, and she felt
strange all over and didn't know why. Her panties felt damp
but it didn't feel like her period starting. For some reason
it made her want to go on thinking about Mark Shigata, and
that really didn't make any sense at all.

*I'll get to them. I'll get to them when the water goes down. For now,
I've got other fish to fry. And look at that sky—*

The man with the binoculars walked back down the dike
toward the condo that looked out over the bay.

*"I told you not to take that stuff. I told you not to take that stuff.
I told you not to take that stuff."*

*"But I didn't take anything and I don't know who you are."
I also don't know where you are. Maybe—*

She'd groped in the wind and the darkness for her shoes,
and like a devil, a demon, a genie out of a bottle, he'd
materialized beside her. "Going somewhere?"

But the wind and the darkness were gone now. They'd
be back, and so would he. But for now, if she could move
fast—

FBI AGENTS, UNLESS THEY'RE ASSIGNED TO THE disaster squad, rarely see the immediate aftermath of violent death. They see it sometimes, of course. More than the average accountant does—a lot of FBI agents are accountants— and more than the average lawyer does—a lot of them are lawyers. But not as much as the average uniform or plain-clothes city cop.

This wasn't the first time Mark Shigata, who only recently had transformed himself from an FBI agent to a small-town cop, had viewed the body of a woman who died violently. It was, without any doubt, however, the messiest.

But just as he'd done the first time he looked at it, a little over an hour ago, he purposefully did not see the ugliness. He forced himself to look for evidence.

"Evidence" is an odd word that means different things to different people. For instance, if a person is convicted only on circumstantial evidence, the man—or woman—in the street wants a retrial. Eyewitness testimony is what really counts, they say.

The average—or above average, or even below average—police officer detests eyewitness testimony. Too often, eyewitness accounts are wrong. Mistaken, deliberately or accidentally. Confused. Misleading.

Circumstantial evidence can be misleading, too, but not nearly so often. People, no matter how well questioned, never tell the whole truth and nothing but the truth because they can't *know* the whole truth, because unadorned truth is impossible for humans to comprehend. Always, in all circumstances, the human mind creates stories, tries to restore order where order has been lost, tries to impose order where there is none. The degree of truth available to humanity is strictly limited, and even where available it is sadly mixed with falsehood.

Physical evidence does a better job in telling the truth. Not the whole truth, but a truth mixed with far less fiction than is possible for the human mind. Things do not lie deliberately, nor do they impose an order that does not exist.

But if the wrong questions are asked, things can distort the truth even more wildly than people. Things answer only the question asked, no matter how seriously off the mark that question is.

Shigata knew how to ask the right questions. Quinn knew enough to recognize where he was ignorant, as did Joel Moran, the investigator from the medical examiner's office.

Jason Southam had taken advantage of the hour or so of relative calm to turn up. He had to have been listening to a police scanner; that was the only way he would have known, because certainly no one had invited him. The power outage had knocked out most of the repeaters, and radio signals weren't carrying very far, but it was Shigata's misfortune that Southam lived in the part of the county that didn't need repeaters to pick up messages on the Bayport police frequency.

Which meant he lived in Bayport, or Texas City, or La-Marque, or one of those little towns in the area. He couldn't have lived on Galveston Island itself, because if he did he'd either be stuck there—there definitely was no traffic across the causeway today—or he'd have been evacuated far enough inland that even in the unlikely event that the scanner would reach that far, he couldn't have gotten to the crime scene.

Jason Southam was an assistant—or associate, or something of that nature—district attorney. He'd been out of law school three months, he'd passed the bar exam two months ago, and he thought he was God.

At least that was Al Quinn's opinion, and Shigata found no reason to argue with him. Quinn expressed the opinion about two minutes after Southam had arrived, when Southam was downstairs examining—and incidentally putting his hands all over—the locked doors and windows. "Didn't it ever cross your mind we might want to fingerprint anything?" Quinn yelled at Southam.

Quinn then stormed upstairs to tell Shigata his opinion. "Can't we get that bastard out of here?" he demanded, not bothering to lower his voice. But then manners weren't Quinn's strong suit at the best of times.

"No," Shigata answered, "we can't. The DA's office has the right to send somebody to a homicide investigation."

"But the DA's office didn't send him," Quinn protested. "He just came."

"True. But he could reasonably argue that the DA's office couldn't send *anybody*."

Southam arrived during the calm, but much later than Shigata and Quinn had, and only minutes before the wall clouds bore down on the coast again. Horizontal rain was now driving through cracks an ant couldn't find, and even inside the house everybody and everything was getting drenched for the second time.

"All right, it was a silly question," Quinn said. "We can't

send him away. Not unless we want him to get blown clean to Beaumont.''

Shigata nodded. Like it or not, he and Quinn, and the suspect and the suspect's brother, and the medical examiner's investigator and the assistant district attorney—and the victim, stiffening on the bed where she'd been killed—weren't going anywhere for a few hours.

Not unless the house went. In which case none of it was going to matter very much, and nobody would ever know any more about who killed Weston's wife than was on the initial report recorded on tape at the police station. And that was provided the station didn't go, which Shigata for one wasn't prepared to bet on. He'd released the few city prisoners on their own recognizance the day before. They couldn't be transported to the county jail on the Island, because the causeway was already closed, and Shigata felt none too secure about the sturdiness of the city jail.

"Oh, shit," Moran muttered.

Nobody had to ask why he said that. Even over the storm, the sound of footfalls on the staircase was quite audible. It wouldn't be either of the Westons; they were both downstairs on the couch, as neither of them seemed to have any inclination whatever to look further at the battered countenance of the late Jean Weston.

Southam paused a moment at the top of the stairs. Then he went into the doorway straight ahead of him. "Oh hell!" Shigata shouted, belatedly realizing what he was doing. "Southam, get out of there."

"I gotta take a leak."

"Not in there!"

But it was too late. He was already doing it, and before Shigata could yell again Southam flushed the toilet.

Southam came out the door. "Now what's the matter with you?"

"Did you happen—just *happen*—to notice a cigarette floating in the toilet?" Shigata asked.

"Yeah. So what?"

"You know whose it was?"

"What difference does that make?"

"Well, it's not mine, because I don't smoke. It's not Quinn's—raising twelve kids on his salary he damn sure doesn't smoke. It's not Weston's or his brother's, because they don't smoke. It's not Jean Weston's, because she didn't smoke. It's not yours or Moran's, because I spotted it before either one of you got here. Now, who do you suppose that leaves?"

Southam didn't answer. He took a comb out of his shirt pocket and carefully ran it through his thin, straight, flaxen hair, an expression of total unconcern on his narrow face. "I don't know. Didn't he say he had a party last night?"

"Yes, there was a party here last night," Shigata agreed. "And don't you think maybe, just maybe possibly, there's this little teeny-weeny chance—"

"About the size of your little teeny-weeny brain," Quinn interposed.

". . . a chance that maybe Dr. Weston and Mrs. Weston might have taken leaks themselves after the party was over? I mean, don't most people go to the bathroom before they go to bed? Especially if they've been drinking heavily during the evening?"

Southam continued to stare.

"You damn fool," Shigata yelled, "that was evidence! There's at least a fifty-fifty chance, maybe better than that, that whoever killed Jean Weston threw that cigarette into the toilet!"

"I doubt that," Southam said patronizingly. "Anyway, even if it was, what difference does flushing it make? So, if that was the murderer's cigarette, then you know the murderer smokes. So what? That doesn't exactly set him apart in any statistically significant way, now does it? I mean, something like forty percent of the adult population—"

"What brand does he smoke?" Quinn asked.

"What?"

"What brand was the cigarette? Did you notice?"

"No, but—"

"It was a Camel. What was his blood type?"

"Now how the hell—"

"A very large percentage of humanity is comprised of what we call secretors," Shigata said. "In a nonsecretor, you can't tell the blood type from things like saliva and semen. In a secretor, you can. Blood type has been determined from the saliva remaining on a discarded cigarette—even after it was discarded in the toilet. You mentioned a forty-percent chance of any given person being a smoker. Well, there's about a seventy-percent chance of any given person being a secretor. Now, if we could say, for example—just for example—that Jean Weston was killed by somebody who smokes Camels and has type AB blood, then that would limit the field just a little, wouldn't it? But you just took care of that for us."

"I don't know what all this fuss is about," Southam said. "I mean, why don't you just arrest Weston?"

"What if he didn't do it?"

"What do you mean, what if he didn't do it? Of course he did."

"How do you know? You ever hear of probable cause? I have no probable cause to arrest Weston. I have no probable cause to assume he did it."

"You don't have to lecture me on law," Southam said, in a rather miffed tone. "I'm an honor graduate of the University of Houston Law School."

"Hooray for you!" Shigata yelled. "I'm an honor graduate of UCLA Law School!"

"What?" Southam said, in a rather different tone of voice.

"I said, I'm an honor graduate of UCLA Law School," Shigata said more quietly. "I've got twenty years of experience in the FBI. I was dealing with the law and with crime scenes—properly—while you were still cutting construction paper in kindergarten. Now listen and hear me well. There was a case a few years ago in Illinois in which the situation was similar to this. And there was a hotshot DA a little like you. And what with one thing and another, a man was railroaded. It's still not a hundred-percent certain he was innocent, but there's a lot better chance he was innocent than that he was guilty. All the same, he did a lot of years in prison and lost his medical license. The state of Illinois looked very, very stupid when it all started coming out. Now, I don't know whether Richard Weston is innocent or guilty. I may never know for sure. Right now I'm leaning to the idea he may have done it. But before I take a warrant, I'm going to be a lot more sure than I am right now. That man is not going to be railroaded. This case is going to be worked right, if I have to pitch you right out the door on your little shell-pink ear. Got it?"

"Yeah, but—"

Shigata eyed Southam, who sputtered into silence.

Shigata turned to Quinn. "Al, you get the camera indoors before the weather closed down again?"

"Ten-four," Quinn answered, looking rather pleased.

The eye was all the way ashore now, heading north. That meant they were back into the worst intensity of the storm. It would last another hour or so at that strength, then gradually the wind would begin to taper off and they would just have to wait for the rain to stop, for the floodwaters to flow into the Gulf, for someone to come and help them change the tire so they could go back home.

Unless the storm did something hurricanes had been known to do before—not often, especially not after the eye had come ashore, but sometimes. Hurricanes don't always move in straight, predictable lines. Sometimes they turn; along the Gulf Coast they often turn east if they're headed north, or north if they're headed west. But sometimes, when they're headed north, they turn west, and sometimes they double back on their tracks.

Melissa hoped this storm would stay on its course. But for some reason she couldn't define, except that she seemed to have some sort of sixth sense where weather was concerned, she had the feeling that it wasn't going to—that it was going to stop, back up into the Gulf, and then return again, passing over again and again until she and Gail were ground into pebbles and washed down into the raging torrent that usually was a country road that ran under and led onto I-45.

"Mommy?" Like a burrowing animal, Gail was digging for comfort. "Mommy, I'm scared." They were both huddled in a blanket, wrapped in the canvas that was supposed to be a tent.

"It's all right, Gail," she said. "It's all right. It's all right."

From here, during the calm, she had been able to see roofs not too far distant. She'd have been able to see the buildings, not just the roofs, if there hadn't been that row of small trees growing on top of the dike. She knew that the roofs belonged to two houses, old ones but nicely remodeled, facing the road—this same road, as it wound around and changed direction—with their backs to the bay.

Then there was a big condominium. A funny kind of place for a condo—you'd expect to find that on Galveston Island facing out to the Gulf, not on the mainland facing the bay and the backside of the Island. But the Island was getting to be not such a good place to live anymore—not if you had children and came equipped with a certain amount of racial prejudice and didn't want to pay for private schools.

Melissa had heard sirens during the calm. Police cars. Mark could be there. So near—not more than a half mile across the field and the dike, maybe a mile and a half by road. She and Gail could walk to him if the storm weren't raging, if the road hadn't turned into an arm of the sea.

The wall cloud seemed to be over them a horribly long time. Longer than it had the first time, before the eye. Was it her imagination, or was it really standing still or beginning to move back out to sea?

The Weston brothers were shouting at each other, and Shigata listened with considerable interest. Southam was upstairs in the bedroom with Quinn and Joel Moran, with orders from Shigata to touch nothing, to watch them work the crime scene, and to ask about anything he didn't understand. Chances were he wasn't going to see much of anything well enough to ask questions. Trying to work a crime scene inside by flashlight is a joke.

At least Southam could hold the flashlight. Even he was competent to do that. What was important was that Southam couldn't hear anything going on downstairs. Shigata scarcely could, and he was sitting on the bottom step.

He wasn't eavesdropping—not exactly. He'd made sure they knew he was there by walking between them to get something out of his briefcase, something he didn't really need but used as an excuse to say without words, "I'm here." They hadn't stopped quarreling. Richard Weston watched Shigata move back to the staircase and sit, before returning his attention to his brother.

Suddenly, there was a tremendous crash directly over-head, so loud they all jumped. The whole house lit up, as every electric bulb blazed on for a second and then as quickly shorted out, as sunlike brilliance shone through the solid walls. For a tiny fraction of a second Shigata felt a burning agony as electricity flashed through the place where a long-ago severe break in his upper left femur had been mended with a metal plate and eight bone screws. At the same time, every hair on his body stood bolt upright.

As quickly as it had come, the burning, the light, and the eerie sensation that he was about to float off the planet vanished altogether.

"That one was close," Dan Weston said, quite calmly. "Richard, I *told* you you need to get lightning rods."

"Yeah, yeah, one of these days."

"One of these days this house is going up and you're going with it." Then Dr. Dan Weston returned to his original chain of thought. "Richard, I'm telling you, you didn't call me. I was here. I didn't go home at all last night. I left the hospital and came over here and I didn't leave again. I slept in Teddy's bed. Don't you remember?"

Dr. Richard Weston shook his head. "I remember that you were going to. But I called you. You answered the phone. You did, Dan."

"Richard, I couldn't have answered the damn phone at my place because I wasn't *at* my place. Look. I'm gonna go through it again. I didn't go to bed Friday night until four o'clock in the morning, because I had a bad emergency surgery. Then I got back up Saturday morning at six, with only two hours of sleep, and I went to the hospital—"

The hospital, Shigata knew, was the University of Texas Medical Branch at Galveston.

"I had three surgeries, all of them emergencies, and I checked on some patients. Then I asked Cal to watch my patients till the storm was over, because he intended to stay on the Island and ride it out. I left the hospital because they were about to close the causeway and I didn't want to get caught on the Island. Then I came here and helped you keep the barbecue going. We had to move the grill into the garage. Now, do you remember all that?"

"I remember all that."

"Then we had the party. Do you remember that?"

"Part of it. I passed out on the couch, so I don't remember the rest of it."

"And *I* remember *that*," Dan agreed. "Okay, then everybody left and Jean went upstairs and went to bed, and I got your shoes off you and then went upstairs to Teddy's room and took my clothes off and went to bed. I'd had a lot to drink and I'd only had two hours of sleep the night before, so I slept hard. I don't remember hearing the storm, but I think it was the eye, the sudden silence, that woke me. Then I got up and found the door broken in." He swallowed. "I went looking for you, and I found Jean. Then I went outside looking for you, and I couldn't find you. By that time I was feeling pretty panicky. I walked partway up to my place, and then I decided there wasn't any reason you'd have gone up there, so I walked back down here and saw you out in the front yard talking to that guy, what's his name, Quinn."

"And you asked me if I did it. I remember that. But I called you on the phone before that and you answered and I said, 'This is Richard. Dan, call the police and get up here fast, they've killed Jean,' and you—damn it, Dan, you *must've* called the police because I sure as hell didn't."

"I didn't call the police. You didn't call me. Look, could you have called the police and *thought* you called me?"

"I know the difference."

Dan Weston turned to Shigata. "What do you think?"

"Well," Shigata said, "I've heard of a lot of people trying to prove they weren't at the place a murder occurred when it occurred. I never yet have heard anybody trying to prove he *was* there at the time. But why didn't you tell Quinn that?"

Dan shook his head. "I don't know. I didn't think of it and he didn't ask me. I guess I assumed he knew I'd been here, and he assumed I was just arriving."

"That does mean I need to ask you some more questions," Shigata pointed out.

"Ask."

He ought to question Dan Weston out of his brother's earshot. But he guessed it didn't make much difference. If they were going to cook up a story together, they'd already had time to do it, and the quarrel they'd just been having was a pretty good indication that they hadn't cooked up anything.

"Do you think your brother would lie to me?" he asked Dan.

Dan shook his head.

He looked at Richard. "Do you think your brother would lie to me?"

"No," Richard said.

"You called your brother. You didn't call the police. That right?"

"That's right."

He swung to face Dan. "You didn't get a phone call from your brother, and you didn't call the police. Is that right?"

"That's right."

"Then who's lying? And who called the police?"

"Does anybody have to be lying?" Dan asked. "Haven't you ever dialed a number from memory and it turned out to be another number you knew just as well? And if that was what happened, the person he called would recognize his voice and would call the police, even if they didn't come over."

"Could that be what happened?" Shigata asked Richard.

Richard shook his head. "I know what number I dialed."

"Are you sure who answered?"

Richard looked surprised. "No. No, I guess I'm not sure. I just heard the one word. Hello. That's all I heard. Then I started talking and then I hung up."

"Is somebody at your house right now?" Shigata asked Dan.

"No. It's locked and boarded up. Anyway, it's not a house, it's a condo."

"So the two of you've told me two diametrically opposite stories, but neither one of you is lying," Shigata said.

After a moment's silence, Dan said, "Sounds like that's about the size of it. You got anything else you want to ask?"

"When you went to bed, who was here?"

"Richard and Jean and me."

"You're positive? Nobody else?"

"Unless somebody was hiding, I'm positive. I mean, I didn't go check all the closets and look under all the beds. But I did lock up."

"You've got a key?"

"I've got a key, yes. I locked up."

Shigata paused. This was making less and less sense. "You woke up after the eye started ashore? The storm wasn't actually blowing when you woke up?"

"That's right."

Shigata looked at Richard. "You broke in the back door to Teddy's room and came in?"

"Right. But I don't know what time that was."

"I do. It was a little after seven," Shigata said. "Carl Moore next door saw you do it. Did you see Dan on Teddy's bed?"

Richard shook his head. "But I don't even know if I looked at Teddy's bed," he answered. "I mean, remember, at this time I hadn't found—found Jean. And Teddy wasn't supposed to be there, I did remember that, and at least temporarily I'd forgotten that Dan was supposed to be. So I don't know if I looked at Teddy's bed at all."

Shigata turned to Dan. "And you didn't wake up? Somebody breaks a door in not six feet from you and you didn't wake up?"

"Obviously not."

"How do you explain that?"

Dan chuckled mirthlessly. "I can tell you were never an intern."

"What does that mean?"

"It means that from six-thirty A.M. Friday to one A.M. Sunday morning—that's about forty-two hours—I had two hours of sleep. Between seven P.M. Saturday and one A.M. Sunday I had about ten drinks. I slept through half of a hurricane. I slept through Richard breaking the door in. I could probably have slept through an earthquake."

"So when you locked up, nobody was here but the three of you, and when you woke up nobody was in the house but you and Jean, and Jean was dead?"

"That's right."

"Why did you think Richard did it?"

"I didn't," Dan said quickly. "I didn't, really," he added. "I just—I guess I just wanted him to tell me he didn't."

"But you woke up and found a door broken in beside the bed you were sleeping in, and your sister-in-law dead, and your brother missing, and your first thought was you wanted to be told he didn't do it?"

"My first thought, after I saw she was definitely dead, my first thought was, I wanted to find him. I thought maybe he was dead too. Then, when I did find him—he wasn't hurt,

but I could see the blood on his pants and shirt—then I—
I told you, I just wanted to be reassured."

"There had to be some reason why you wanted to be reassured."

"Quit badgering him," Richard said, in a perfectly reasonable tone of voice. "He doesn't want to tell you and I already did. We'd been fighting, Jean and I."

"What about?" Shigata asked.

Both the Westons started to speak at once and then both fell silent, trying to defer to each other.

"You know you don't have to answer me," Shigata remarked.

"We know that," Richard said. "Actually, I think Dan does, though. I mean, he's not the suspect, so doesn't he have to answer you?"

"Not anymore," Shigata said. "Not since he told me he spent the night in this house. In fact"—Shigata stood up, walked through the living room between the men again, stumbling in the near-total darkness, and opened his briefcase—"I should have done this as soon as you said that." He produced a Miranda form and started explaining what it said.

"I know what it says," Dan interrupted. "I watch cop shows on TV whenever I have time." By the light of the one small utility candle they had been able to find in the house, Dan signed the form and passed it over to Richard to witness. "Now I don't have to answer," Dan said.

"But just in case you decide to, what were Richard and Jean fighting over?"

"Not fighting," Richard said quickly. "Just arguing."

"You want me to answer?" Dan asked him.

Richard nodded. "You might as well. Look, Chief Shigata, try to understand this. I guess everybody you arrest, everybody you talk to, says, 'I didn't do it,' and I guess you've learned to listen to that the way I listen to the patient with AIDS and severe anal lesions who says he's not gay and gosh, he just doesn't know where he got such an awful disease. But every now and then I get somebody who's got AIDS and isn't gay and doesn't do drugs. And every now and then you get somebody who says he's innocent and really is. Well, whether you believe it or not, I'm that one. I did not kill my wife. Some of what you're going to dig out isn't going to make me look like the most outstanding citizen in the world. That's because I'm not the most outstanding citizen in the world. I have a high-stress profession and I act like an ass off-duty to try to keep the stress from killing me. All the same, I did not kill my wife. I'm going to do my damnedest to make sure you find out everything you possibly can about me and Jean, because I figure that's the only way you're ever going to find out who did it.

"I don't like my patients hiding facts from me, and I won't hide facts from you," Richard said. "Besides, I don't want anybody to think I did it. So, yeah, Dan, tell him the truth. Frankly, I'm not even sure I remember all of it. Just that we were quarreling."

"You were quarreling about the baby."

"What baby? Oh, you mean the baby that Jean's—that Jean was going to have? Was that really what we were quarreling about?"

"Yeah," Dan said. "You kept saying it wasn't yours."

"What the hell would I say that for?" Richard demanded. "Of course it was mine." He appealed again to Shigata. "Of course the baby was mine."

"*In vino veritas,*" Shigata murmured. "When you're drunk your subconscious talks as much as your conscious self does. You ought to know that."

"I do know that. But I don't know why I would say the

baby wasn't mine." He turned to Dan. "Whose did I say it was?"

Dan shook his head. "You didn't say. You just kept insisting it wasn't yours. It was pretty embarrassing to listen to. I started to go home when everybody else did."

"Why didn't you?" Shigata said.

Dan shook his head again. "I guess I decided it might not be such a good idea."

"In case I wanted to wake up and resume the argument?" Richard asked. Dan nodded.

"I've never been violent, even when I was drunk."

"Except that once."

"That was twenty years ago in Acapulco," Richard said quickly.

"I'm not trying to set you up," Dan said. "It's just that it's on record."

"It was still only once. You know I've never hit Jean."

"That's true," Dan said. "You never have. And there's been a time or two I would've been tempted to, if she was mine."

Richard Weston started shaking his head and forgot to stop. "This doesn't make one damn bit of sense," he said. "Not any sense at all."

This doesn't make any sense at all.

She wasn't so dizzy now. And he'd half-boarded up the window from the inside, since he couldn't get at it from the outside. It wasn't totally secure, but there wasn't so much wind and rain getting inside as there had been.

She forced herself to stay on track. She'd gotten home. She was supposed to be gone for another week, but she heard about the storm. That would cause a lot of injuries, and she was conscientious. Of course, she couldn't get to the hospital right now, because there would be no way to get across the causeway, but as soon as the storm was over and they started letting traffic through, she'd get right to work.

So she went home, one car driving south past that long caravan of cars going north. She got home about midnight or something like that. She went upstairs and—there they all were. Dead. She'd seen death before, a lot of it, more than most young women of twenty-four, but this was not impersonal death to her, this was personal death, her home, her friends.

She panicked. She ran out and tried to get in the car, but in just the few seconds she was inside somebody had opened the hood of her car. It was open when she got outside; someone had yanked some wires loose so she couldn't start the engine.

Whoever he was, whoever did that, was still out there.

She didn't have a gun. She didn't have anything. So she got out of the car and ran for safety. There was the condo —*his* condo—she'd be safe there.

It had been a couple of weeks since she'd been inside, but he couldn't have changed the combination on the lock that fast. She pushed the four numbers on the panel in the right sequence—she hoped it was the right sequence—and she pushed the door open. She saw someone standing in the darkness and she fell inside screaming, "Thank God you're here—"

It wasn't him.

This was his condo, but he wasn't here. That other one was.

It didn't make any sense at all.

"**Y**OU GOTTA BE KIDDING," QUINN SAID AT the end of Shigata's rather comprehensive recital. "Both of them? Here all night?"

"Both of them," Shigata answered wearily. "Here all night. Dan Weston swears he slept through the whole thing. And each one says the other one has to have been the one that called the station because *he* sure as hell didn't."

"Somebody called the station."

"We'll find out who eventually. If the station doesn't blow away, that is."

"How do you plan on doing that?"

"Cut out that section of the dispatch tape and send it to Austin with tapes of both of them. Ask for voice prints." Some previous Bayport chief of police had managed to get a federal grant for a sophisticated tape-recording system, so that all incoming telephone calls to either the listed police department number or the 911 emergency number were recorded. This wouldn't be the first time Shigata had found the system useful.

"So that takes care of that," Quinn said.

"That takes care of that. What I'm concerned about at

this moment is what we can do here and now. I checked Weston—Dan Weston, that is. He hasn't got a drop of blood anywhere, except on his shoes. His clothes are completely clean, and not any wetter than they ought to be, all things considered."

Shigata and Quinn were standing on the upstairs deck, the only place they could think of where they could feel reasonably certain Southam couldn't eavesdrop. Of course, that also meant they were both getting more and more drenched, but it wasn't a whole lot drier indoors.

"You saw that room in there," Quinn said, nodding toward it. The Westons' bedroom didn't have a door to the deck, but it did have a window, covered by a frilly white curtain now splotched with darkening blood, as was the inside of the window pane itself.

Shigata nodded.

"Whatever he was swinging, he was splashing blood everywhere," Quinn said. "It had to get on him."

"It got on him," Shigata said. "I can tell where he was standing. Can you?"

Quinn thought about it.

The room was a funny shape. It had started out a large square, a very large room indeed. But all four corners had been bitten out by smaller squares, so that the door into the hall and the three large windows were all enclosed in alcoves. The northwest alcove adjacent to the upstairs deck held the queen-size bed, its head square to the window, and a large bachelor dresser. There wasn't much walk space to spare on either side of the bed. The southwest alcove, by the side window, held the television set. A long dresser was set in the southeast alcove, by the front window. The northeast alcove held built-in shelving and the stereo on its long wall.

The two corners along the southwest wall were taken up

with built-in clothes closets; the southeast corner, at the inside front, was the entrance into the long closet that led between the two bedrooms; and the northeast corner, at the inside back, surrounded part of the bathroom.

The house was built before air-conditioning, and the arrangement would have been completely absurd anyplace except near the beach, where every possible breath of cross-ventilation was needed. In this milieu, the design made sense. It would be a bright, airy room, comfortable and welcoming, if all the windows except the one over the deck had not been boarded up because of the hurricane, and if the room had not reeked with blood.

Jean Weston's body was on the bed, faceup, with her head almost directly under the window that opened onto the deck. She was on the left side of the bed—the southwest side, toward the outside wall. To reach her, the killer had to be standing on the left side of the bed, inside the alcove.

Blood had splashed all over the alcove, but a lot more on the left side than the right. Some of it—not much, because the room was very large—had splashed out into the center area, where the lounge chairs were.

It appeared that whoever killed her had struck her repeatedly, more times than it would be possible to count even in the autopsy. With each blow, the blood splashed toward the killer, toward the wall behind him, over his head, around him on both sides.

There was one area, partly on the side of the dresser and partly on the wall, where there was very little blood—roughly the size of a man crouching—crouching as he would have to have been to strike a sleeping woman repeatedly on the head.

Quinn opened his eyes, not realizing until then that he had closed them while he was visualizing the scene. "Yes," he said. "Yes, I know where he was standing. Man, he had blood all over him."

"Head to foot," Shigata agreed. "But the problem is he could have been naked when he did it. Or for that matter, no matter what he had on, all he had to do was step outdoors about three seconds and wash clean in that downpour. So what've we got? We've got Dan Weston completely clean and not completely wet. We've got Richard Weston with one splash of blood on his shoulder, which is too much if he did go out in the rain after it, because it would have washed out, and too little if he didn't go out in the rain. But we know he *did* go out in the rain, because his next-door neighbor *saw* him out in the rain, and Jean Weston couldn't possibly have been killed after that. There's just not enough time for the body to reach its present condition if she was. Richard Weston also had one smudge on his knee, which he probably got exactly the way he says he did, because that one place on the bed where he says he put his knee when he was checking on her has sand on it and smells of seawater."

"And they both tracked all over the bedroom," Quinn said, "so footprints aren't going to do us any good at all."

"There's one problem with all this, you know."

"What's this?"

"About ninety-nine times out of a hundred, when you get this kind of an onslaught that just doesn't ever stop, it was a woman who did it."

"You gotta be kidding," Quinn said.

"Uh-uh. You get an ax murder, something like that, it's nearly always a woman. Usually a sweet, demure little thing, you'd think butter wouldn't melt in her mouth. Or if it's not, then it's a male—man or boy—who *feels* weak, feels defenseless. Can't stop because if he stops that corpse is gonna get right off that bed and go after him. You see what I mean?"

"Yeah," Quinn said. "I should have remembered. There was that case up around Plano a few years back. A woman killed her friend—whacked her to splinters with an ax—and then took the friend's kids to a swimming party. Sat down next to a police-department secretary, and the secretary noticed a cut on her foot where the ax had slipped and asked about it and she managed to cover up. Of course, the secretary remembered it later. Only problem is, we haven't got a woman in this case."

"Yet," Shigata said. "And you're right, we may not. There are always exceptions."

"Oh, shit," Quinn said, changing the subject slightly. "You figure out what she was hit with?"

"I think so," Shigata said. "You?"

"I think so," Quinn said. "What do you think?"

"You go first."

"You're the smart guy that's been to college and all the FBI schools. You go first."

Shigata shrugged. "A six-cell metal flashlight with a flaring lens guard."

"Why a six-cell?"

"A two-cell or four-cell wouldn't have been heavy enough. What do you think?"

"I came to the same conclusion. That lens guard would cut like an ax, if you hit hard enough with it."

"Only it'd leave curved cuts."

"And curved cuts is what we've got." Quinn paused a beat. "Besides that, I found one."

"One what? Six-celled metal flashlight?"

"Yeah. Down on the beach."

"Near the keys?"

Quinn shook his head. "Not very near. Near enough it

could have been pitched from there by somebody with a good arm, but I sort of don't think it was. More like somebody was walking away and dropped it."

"Any blood on it?"

"Some. It had been rained on, a lot, but some blood had gotten inside the lens. The lens is cracked. There's blood in the crack and some actually inside."

"You said walking on the beach. Which way?"

"North," Quinn said, meaning northeast. The beach at that point ran almost exactly northeast-southwest. Up the coast, toward Houston, was north, even if at some particularly serpentine curve of beach it happened in fact to be south. Down the coast, toward Brownsville, was south.

Shigata nodded. "Okay. That's something to keep in mind."

"That's where the condos are."

"Dan Weston lives in a condo."

"There are a lot of condos in Galveston County," Quinn pointed out.

"True, but Dan said he started to walk from here to his condo. There's only one group of condos in reasonable walking distance from here."

"Nice," Quinn said. "Nice, nice, nice. So the Westons—Richard and Jean—were fighting about whose the baby was."

"So says Dan."

"But Richard didn't say whose he thought it was."

"Again, so says Dan."

"What if Richard said it was Dan's?"

"Then Dan wouldn't want to tell us that. But in that case why would he tell us they were fighting over the baby at all?"

"Maybe because he figured somebody else would tell us."

"Possibly," Shigata said. "But in that case the somebody else could also tell us whose baby Richard says it was."

"Not if the fight went on after everybody else left."

"Do you like that scenario?"

"Not without knowing a lot more about Dan Weston," Quinn said. "Where's his wife? Dan's, I mean?"

"He's divorced," Shigata said. "I did get that."

"Girlfriend?"

"He says so. He says he's shacked up with an intern—"

"Intern?" Quinn said, eyebrows raised.

"They come in both genders now," Shigata pointed out. "He showed me her picture. Let's say if you had her you wouldn't be too likely to look elsewhere. Now, I ask again. You like that scenario?"

"No," Quinn confessed. "It makes a real good story, but I don't feel like it's what happened."

"Me neither. Oh, shit. I wish we had a better idea when she died."

"There's not much rigor yet."

"Well, there wouldn't be," Shigata replied. "We know she was alive at midnight. But there wasn't much postmortem staining, either, when I got here."

"I noticed that too," Quinn said.

As long as a person is living, the heart continues to drive the blood, but as soon as the heart stops, the blood begins to pool at the lowest part of the body. A twelve-hour corpse will be nearly pallid in the uppermost areas, while the underside will be mulberry-purple with postmortem staining, or postmortem lividity, hypostasis.

Judging by the degree of hypostasis, Jean Weston hadn't been dead twelve hours when the police arrived, and probably hadn't been dead much more than six hours. She could have been killed at six in the morning, maybe as late as seven, certainly not much earlier than five.

Which meant that whoever killed her was already in the house when she went to bed at one or so in the morning, and was probably still in the house at this moment, unless he—or she—came in through a hurricane and left through a hurricane.

There was one problem with that whole theory, and Quinn pointed it out. "There's not much staining now, either," he said. "And there's not going to be. She damn near bled dry."

"I should have thought of that," Shigata muttered. "Damn it, what've we got to go on? We can't do much by temperature because it's like an oven in there. She's not going to go much below normal body temp no matter how long she's been dead, if ambient temp is normal body temp."

"So what've we got? We've got a dead woman. We don't know when she died. We know who was in the house with her when she died, but it doesn't really look like either of them did it. We can't get out to ask anybody else any questions, but it wouldn't do much good if we could because the chances of anybody else knowing anything useful are just about zilch."

"You got any chewing gum?" Shigata asked.

"What do you want chewing gum for?" Quinn demanded, producing an opened package of Wrigley's from his pants pocket.

"I don't. I want a cigarette."

"Resist the urge," Quinn advised. "This is the damnedest murder I ever worked." He leaned back against the main wall of the house.

"How many murders have you worked?" Shigata inquired.

Quinn straightened. "As many as you have, unless you worked some I don't know about."

"The FBI doesn't have primary jurisdiction in a murder case unless it's on federal land."

"What does that mean?"

"I've worked a few more than you have, but not many more."

"Am I dreaming, or is the rain slowing down?"

"You're dreaming," Shigata said. "What the hell are they quarreling about now?" He headed for Teddy's bedroom, to get back into the house.

It seemed to be clearing in the north. Through the still-pouring rain he could see occasional glimpses of blue sky.

There was something funny about that. The worst of the hurricane ought to have been about over by now. It ought to be tapering off. But not so clear yet. And it should be tapering off to the south, as the storm moved north.

So what did that mean, a partial clearing in the north?

One thing it meant was he could take the binoculars and walk down and look at that blond under the bridge again. Look at her again and think what he was going to do with her, when he could get to her. Wonder whether he wanted to get out a boat and try to get to her before anybody else did, or wait until the road was passable again and anybody could get down there, and hope he got there first.

He'd figured out why she was there. Looking through the binoculars, he'd been able to see the car by the service station, and he'd been able to see that its tire was flat. But that didn't mean she couldn't change it. It wasn't very ladylike to change a tire, but all the same it seemed like a lot of women did it.

But she wouldn't be able to get out before he got in. Her car was a little tail-dragger; he had a pickup truck he'd jacked up onto big tires. So he could get to her through the water a long time before she could get away without drowning her car completely.

In the meantime, he'd have to think what to do with the one in here. He didn't know her name but that didn't matter; he knew she was one of Them because she couldn't have gotten in here if she wasn't.

He wasn't ready to kill her yet. He was thinking about how he was going to kill her. He'd decide for sure a little later. For now, he'd just feed her some happy pills. Then she'd go to sleep while he went down and looked at the other one.

He went to the medicine cabinet, where he'd found the happy pills. Valium, ten milligrams. One of them ought to be enough to knock her cold. He'd feed her five, just in case. After a moment's thought, he emptied the contents of several assorted capsules into a glass of water and stirred until it all dissolved.

He took her the pills and the water. "I told you not to take that stuff," he told her.

"What stuff?" she asked. "I didn't take anything but what you gave me."

"You took some more stuff after that. That's why you have a headache."

"No I didn't. I couldn't have. Anyway, how do you know I have a headache?"

"Just take this now. It'll help you feel better. Get rid of that headache."

She looked at the pills. "That's ten-milligram Valium."

She knew without seeing the bottle, he noted. Of course, she would, if she was one of Them.

"That's right," he said.

"It won't make me feel better. Anyway, I don't have a headache." That was a lie. She did have a headache.

"Yes, it will."

"You want me to take five of them? That's crazy. That's fifty milligrams of Valium. Nobody needs—"

"It'll make you feel better."

"But—"

"It'll make you feel a lot better," he said, "than if I stick this knife in you."

She stared at him. She thought about the scene she'd walked into, in the middle of the night. And she put the Valium tablets in her mouth and swallowed water.

Satisfied, he left. Gwen spat the soggy, partially dissolved Valium tablets into her hand. She grabbed for Kleenex and wiped the inside of her mouth, rinsed her mouth with the glass of water he'd left, wiped her mouth again, and finally drank some water.

She knew she'd swallowed some of it. She didn't know how much, but maybe she'd gotten rid of enough of it that she'd be able to stay awake, when he did whatever it was he didn't want her to be awake for.

"Mommy, the sun's coming out!" Gail said.

"It is, isn't it?" Melissa agreed.

"Is it going to stay this time, or is it just for a little while again?"

"I'm afraid it's just for a little while again." The hot stickiness of the eye of the storm was back, but the sunshine had come from the north. Melissa hoped Gail hadn't realized what that meant.

They were going to be stranded here a lot longer, and they were nearly out of food.

The only possible source of food was the vending machines at the service station, and since they were run on electricity, the only way to get anything out of them was with a crowbar. And even if Melissa could manage to get them open, which she considered highly doubtful, there wasn't anything there except peanuts and potato chips and corn chips and cheese crisps, all of which would make them even thirstier, and that remaining gallon of water hadn't been meant to last this long.

"You are not going to take any aspirin, if I have to take it away from you and flush it down the toilet!" Dan Weston yelled.

"Dan, it's a headache," his brother replied. "A plain old garden-variety headache. That's all. There's no reason—"

"If you got hit in the head and you insist on taking aspirin you'll start bleeding."

"I didn't get hit in the head! I know where I got hit. I got hit in the shoulder, and I think I have a cracked clavicle, but I did not get hit in the head. Don't you think I know where I got hit?"

"Richard, use your head! You know what aspirin can do to somebody with a concussion. At least let me have a look at you."

"I have a hangover," Richard said carefully. "I woke up with a hangover to find out my wife had been murdered. Now, if you don't think that's enough reason to have a headache—"

"Let me check your head, and if I don't find anything I'll give the aspirin back," Dan proposed.

Richard shrugged and began to work his fingers, with evident knowledge of what he was feeling for, over his own head. Then he paused, stiffened, lowered his hand and looked at it. Even from where he was standing several feet away in the near darkness, Shigata could see on Richard Weston's hand flakes of glossy-black dried blood.

"What do you know?" Weston said, a certain tone of surprise in his voice. "I did get hit in the head."

"Let me see." Dan Weston started checking. "Yeah,

you've got a hell of a knot there. Certainly at least a mild concussion, possibly a slight fracture. You need an X ray.''

Richard shrugged. "Okay. You win. No aspirin.''

"How'd you know he had a concussion?" Quinn asked.

"I can see his eyes. He can't. That's all.''

"Where on the shoulder were you hit?" Shigata asked.

"Here,'' Richard said, indicating the spot of the left shoulder where the splash of blood began. From there it sprayed down and in, ending right where the shirt buttoned, about seven inches above the waist.

Quinn and Shigata looked at each other. "Can you open the shirt and let me see if there's any visible bruising yet?" Shigata asked.

"I guess,'' Richard said, sounding puzzled.

The bruise was the arc of a large circle—about thirty degrees of arc.

Quinn, experimentally, moved his right hand back toward his own shoulder, as if testing a possible blow. He tried it again left-handed. Then he shook his head and looked at Shigata.

"You can't do it,'' Shigata said. "Which means he couldn't do it.''

"So that's that,'' Quinn said. "That's why the blood didn't wash out. After the son of a bitch coldcocked him, he laid in here unconscious long enough for the blood to dry. *Then* he went outside.''

Both Westons had said they'd slept part of the night in Teddy Weston's bed, but there were twin beds in Teddy Weston's room. Had Richard Weston been too drunk, too stunned from the blow, to know which bed he landed in? Did Dan Weston, who after all didn't live here, actually know which bed was Teddy's and which was the spare bed? On both counts, maybe—but maybe not.

"You've decided I didn't do it," Richard Weston said, watching them intently.

"And now you think I did," Dan Weston added.

"On the face of the evidence, isn't that a fairly reasonable theory?" Shigata asked.

"As long as it stays a theory," Dan Weston said. "But don't make it a supposition, because I didn't. And I want to get him to the hospital while we can. There's not much time to do it. We better leave now. We ought to be able to get on to Mainland Center Hospital from here before the storm closes in again."

"I'll take you," Shigata said. "I've got four-wheel drive."

"And you don't want to let the suspects out of your sight," Dan Weston challenged.

Shigata shrugged. "Put it that way if you want to. Quinn'll keep the roof on here. And Mr. Southam was just leaving, weren't you, Mr. Southam?"

It appeared that Jason Southam was just leaving. It also appeared he wasn't too happy about it.

The quickest way to the Mainland Center Hospital was the freeway, which would certainly be passable. But getting to the freeway might be another matter. Weston's house faced roughly northwest on a road that, like the beach, ran roughly northeast-southwest. But the road, unlike the beach, ran in that direction only a little way. Then it abruptly curved almost due north, to run at an angle under the freeway, which ran north-northeast at this point. There was an Exxon station at that point on one corner, and not much of anything else.

Shigata headed up that road for about fifty yards. Then he stopped, studied the surface of the water and the road markers, and made a U-turn.

"What are you doing?" Dan Weston asked.

"I'm not driving a submarine," Shigata replied. "We're going to have to make it on surface streets."

Making the trip on surface streets required a lot of backing up and detouring. Shigata got on the radio to ask what streets were passable, but the dispatchers didn't know much more than he did.

"This milk tastes yucky," Joey complained.

"It's all the milk there is," Steve answered.

"It makes my tummy hurt. I want Kool-Aid instead."

"We don't have any Kool-Aid."

"I want *Mommy!*" Joey wailed.

"She'll come back."

"I want to go find Mommy!"

"Mommy told us to stay home till she got back," Steve said firmly. "And we've got to do it."

But Mommy never stayed away this long before. It was yesterday she went to the laundromat. All the clocks are stopped, but it's got to be past time for school to be out if we had school today. And we've had the hurricane. She was going to get the washing done before the hurricane. She said so. That was why she went out when she did.

Something's wrong.

He'd left. Gwen had feigned sleep, keeping her breathing steady while he watched her to make sure she was asleep, while she watched him with half-closed eyes. He was carrying a hunting knife in a sheath at his belt and wearing binoculars on a strap around his neck. He left, closing the door behind him.

She waited a few minutes to be sure he wouldn't come back and try to catch her awake. Then she got up, very quietly in case he was outside, put on her shoes, and went to see if the keys to the pickup truck were where they usually were. She knew this condo as well as she knew her own apartment. The car keys were gone, as she'd expected them to be, but the pickup keys were there.

She was afraid to go out a door, so she went out a window and down the wet fire escape. At the bottom of the fire escape, jammed back between it and the wall, was a quantity of wood—then he *had* boarded up. The other one had removed the boards.

Why? That seemed an awfully strange thing to do.

"Mommy!" Gail said. "There's a man watching us."

"I see him," Melissa said. "Why don't you wave at him?" She waved herself, feeling a fool but wanting to jolly Gail out of her unusual timidity.

"I don't want to. I don't like him."

"Gail, that's silly, you don't even know him. See, he's waving back."

"I don't like him, anyway." Reluctantly, she waved. "Is he going to come help us?"

"He can't get to us."

"Maybe he could get a boat."

"Not through that current," Melissa said. "Try not to worry, baby. We'll get out of here eventually." He lowered his binoculars.

I'll get them. I'll get them soon. This is right, the plan. Not to kill Them, but to kill Their women, leave Them as alone as I am. Even that little one is a wanton. Look at her, waving like that when she doesn't even know me.

"I'm surprised you're not asking questions," Richard Weston remarked after a while.

"Do you want me to ask questions?" Shigata asked.

"Not especially. I'm just surprised you're not. I mean, people are usually more off-guard in this type of situation."

"So you'll be more truthful? I thought you said you were truthful to start with."

"I am."

"Actually, I do have a question," Shigata said, "but it doesn't have anything to do with this. You're a neurosurgeon, right?"

"Right," both Westons said at once.

"Okay, well, a while ago you were talking about patients with AIDS. So how does a neurosurgeon happen to be treating AIDS cases? It seems like it would fall out of your area of expertise."

"It does," Richard Weston said. "But there's something a lot of people don't know about AIDS. The AIDS virus attacks the brain. Most often, you find the problems in full-blown cases of AIDS, but sometimes you get the mental problems with no other overt symptoms at all except a positive ELISA. A few years back, before anybody knew much of anything about AIDS, when we were still trying to figure out what was going on, these people would come in with obvious brain damage, and they'd be referred to neurosurgeons, because right then all anybody knew was there was a person with brain damage and nobody knew if it was a stroke, a blood clot, or what. So I got a few cases referred to me."

"Was there anything you could do about it?"

"Nothing at all," Richard said. "Sometimes it was really tragic. I had one case—a fairly young woman, early forties. She'd had cancer. The cancer itself wasn't too bad as cancers go, I think she'd have gotten over it completely. But this was before anybody had any idea how AIDS spread. In fact, I think it started before we quite knew there was any such disease as AIDS. Anyhow, this woman had been given a couple of blood transfusions and apparently one of them was tainted with the virus. She'd also been given chemotherapy, so her immune system was considerably weakened. She had a full-blown case of AIDS in just about six months, and it went straight to her brain. There wasn't anything anybody could do but just watch her die. It was—not a good situation. You remember, Dan?"

"I remember. We both worked on it. It was a pretty bad mess. Her husband and son were both—I don't even want to think about it."

"Did they sue you?"

"No," Richard said. "I think the son wanted to. The husband didn't. He knew it wasn't anything we could have prevented. Anyway, we didn't give the transfusion, her oncologist did that. Hey, aren't we in LaMarque?"

"We are," Shigata said. "I ran out of streets in Bayport and Texas City."

There was a roadblock ahead—not wooden barricades, which would certainly blow away, but two police cars, which might not. "Damn," Shigata said. "If we don't get through this one, we may not get through at all." He pulled up, and one of the officers, in a yellow slicker, strolled up beside him. Shigata pulled out his ID and held it out the window.

"H'lo, Chief," the patrolman said. "Shigata? Bayport?"

"Shigata, Bayport," Shigata confirmed. "Is this road passable at all? I've got a possible skull fracture."

"You've got a—"

"In the back seat," Shigata amended.

"That does make a little bit of difference," the officer drawled. "Yeah, it's passable. You've just got to stay in the exact center of the road. Both sides are shoulder-deep on me."

"And it looks like you've been in it."

"I've been in it," the officer said. "About six times. That's why we set up the barricade. I've had to fish several people out. They try to go to the hospital and they get stuck."

"So can we get to the hospital?"

"Oh, yeah, you can get there, as long as you stay in the middle of the road. But watch out for the emergency-room parking lot. It's flooded."

"Thanks," Shigata said, and drove around the police cars, carefully staying in the middle of the street.

From that intersection, it normally took five minutes to drive to the hospital. This time it took twenty-five minutes, and the black wall clouds were closing in again from the north by the time Shigata parked the car.

The hospital's admissions clerk looked harassed. "You'll have to wait until we can get to you," she said. "We're doing the best we can, but—" She gestured at the waiting room.

The emergency room was about as full as it could get. Two women were in labor. There had been several dozen car wrecks. One man was getting two hundred stitches in his arm; listening to the conversation, Shigata deduced that the man had been in his front yard in thong sandals when the last wall cloud closed in, had tried to run indoors and lost one of his sandals, and had fallen through a plate-glass window that should have been boarded up. Somebody else was there with apparent appendicitis, being readied for X ray.

It was going to be a while.

"I'm a doctor myself," Dan said to the clerk. "In fact, we're both doctors. If somebody can get me a gurney, at least I can get him lying down, and then I could help out here while we're waiting to get him into X ray."

"Yes, sir, we'll see. We do have one room—" "Doctors" was apparently the magic word. The Westons followed the nurse.

A young woman burst through the door. How she'd managed to get in Shigata didn't want to try to guess—the wind had to be a hundred and fifty miles an hour, and she didn't look like she weighed a hundred pounds. Her blond hair was a dripping mess, her clothes drenched, and her face chalk white. She took two steps into the waiting room and dropped to the floor before Shigata could get there to catch her.

By the time a nurse arrived to help, her eyes were open again. "He killed them!" she said, in a very loud and clear voice. "He killed them! I got there and found them and he wouldn't let me leave. He kept me—"

There was a sudden commotion down the hall. Dan Weston, minus his brother, was running back toward the waiting room. Shigata turned to face him, wondering if Richard's condition had suddenly worsened, but Dan wasn't looking at Shigata. "Gwen!" he shouted. "Gwen, what the hell—"

"Danny, he killed them!" she shouted back. She tried to sit up and fainted again.

FIRST-COME, FIRST-SERVED IS NOT A RULE THAT applies in emergency rooms. Someone whose needs are slight might wait for hours, while doctors and nurses attend to newly incoming patients with greater needs.

They call it triage, a practice developed out of necessity by army doctors. Those with serious injuries who are likely to survive are helped first. Next come those with slighter injuries; they are likely to survive. Those with serious injuries and an extremely slim likelihood of survival are helped last, if at all, depending on the availability of personnel.

Thus, Dr. Richard Weston, who had a possible skull fracture but who had walked in under his own power, was waiting. An accident victim brought in by ambulance, with a flat brain-wave pattern and gray oatmeal-looking tissue oozing from a visibly crushed skull, was waiting, although he had been placed decently out of sight to die as quietly and humanely as possible. Meanwhile, doctors and nurses rushed to an unknown young woman in the entryway, unconscious for unknown reasons.

One of the doctors was Richard Weston, who had jumped

THE EYE OF ANNA

off the gurney he had been placed on to head for the commotion. Some doctors are as bad as cops, Shigata thought.

Dan Weston scolded his errant brother furiously. "Get yourself back down!" he shouted. "Haven't I got enough to worry about?"

"Yeah, but that's Gwen."

"I can take care of Gwen!"

He couldn't, of course. Nobody could take care of Gwen adequately, until somebody figured out what was wrong with her.

Shigata stayed out of the way. This was not his area of expertise. What was, in part, his area of expertise was keeping extraneous people out of the way, and that he did as much as anybody could.

The waiting room was complete pandemonium. It was small, meant to hold at the most ten or twelve people. The emergency room itself had only four beds. In a pinch, four or five more people could be squeezed into beds, gurneys, or stretchers in the hall.

Right now, twenty-odd people had crowded themselves into the waiting room, sitting in the chairs, sprawling on the floor, pacing aimlessly. The line for the one available telephone was a constant five or six people long, but almost no calls could get out. People hung up, looking disgusted or angry, to be followed by other hopefuls.

Some children were scampering around, occasionally being corralled by parents, but the minute the parents turned their attention away the children resumed their antics. Some children weren't scampering; one sat listlessly in his mother's lap, his head pressed to her breast, and even from across the room Shigata could see the flush of fever on the little face. But triage counted here, too, so they'd get to him when they could.

Until they moved somebody into a regular hospital room

or back into the waiting area, there wasn't any place to put Gwen—whoever Gwen was, and whatever was wrong with her.

"Danny," she said urgently. "Danny. Danny. He wouldn't let me leave. But when he went away I got out."

"Who wouldn't let you leave?" Dan Weston asked, his hands moving over her head, checking, probing for damage.

"Danny. Danny."

"I'm Danny," Dan Weston said. "I'm here." He held her head still for a moment, gazing into her eyes more professionally than romantically.

"Danny, he killed them!" Or was it, "Danny! He killed them!"

"Who killed who?" Dan Weston asked in an absent-minded voice, still checking her head.

"Danny! In my apartment!" Her head dropped to the side again, eyes flickering and then closing.

"She hasn't got any kind of knot on her head," Dan said. "She looks like she might've had an OD."

"What would she be taking?" a nurse asked. "And what's her name?"

"Her name's Gwen. And she doesn't take things."

Richard Weston arrived again, pushing the gurney meant for him. "Let's get her on this," he said. "At least we can see what we're doing."

"Gwen?" the nurse said in a loud voice. "Gwen, can you hear me?"

"How the hell did she get here?" Richard Weston asked his brother.

Dan shook his head. "Damned if I know. Nurse, can we get some blood samples? Find out what it was she took?"

A black man dressed far more like a doctor than either of the Westons was at this time shouldering his way between

Dan and Gwen. "Who do you think you are?" he demanded, glaring at Dan.

"Daniel Weston. Neurosurgeon. UTMB."

"You practice in this hospital?" the man demanded, not seeming at all mollified by Dan's nervous professional courtesy.

"No, I told you I practice in the University of Texas Medical Branch in Galveston."

"Then get the hell out of my way!" the doctor roared, and began giving orders while Dan, looking somewhat startled, backed out of his way and Richard sat down on the floor in a corner until somebody could arrive with a new gurney.

The doctor ordered blood and urine tests—it would take about twenty minutes to get the results, if the emergency power didn't go off. While they were waiting, she would be taken for full skull X rays. In the meantime, they were starting an IV drip to try to dilute whatever was in her bloodstream that didn't belong there.

The admissions clerk now managed to corral Dan Weston, on the grounds that he seemed to know her, and Shigata prepared to listen. Almost certainly, everything the clerk wanted to know, Shigata wanted to know also.

Her name was Gwen Hardesty. She was twenty-four, and Shigata knew from the address that she lived in a reconverted old house near the condo where Dan Weston lived. She was an intern at UTMB. Dan didn't—or said he didn't—have any idea when or how she had come about her injury or overdose.

Shigata wasn't sure he believed that.

The nurse went on asking questions about insurance and so forth that Shigata didn't need the answers to. He backed off, to pull his notebook out and draw a rough map on a sheet of paper.

Bayshore Road runs roughly northeast-southwest. There aren't many houses on it. People with a lot of money generally don't want to look at Galveston Bay, the back side of Galveston Island, Bolivar Peninsula, or the Intracoastal Waterway. They want to look at the Gulf of Mexico. And if you didn't have a lot of money, you couldn't afford the high tolls exacted by the many floods that hit the immediate area.

So Bayshore Road contained a house, its back to the Bay, the property of Richard Weston. It had a group of condominiums—brick, which was absurd in this climate—about ten dwellings in all if Shigata remembered correctly, one of which was occupied, and probably owned, by Dan Weston. It had one more house, rather large frame, painted an unfortunately garish blue, which had been remodeled into three apartments, the largest of which was occupied by a varying group of female interns and residents at UTMB.

All very convenient if the Weston brothers wanted to spend a lot of time together. All very convenient if Dan Weston wanted his girlfriend near him but not living with him.

Weston was through answering questions. He'd gone to check on his brother and/or his girlfriend and/or the emergency-room doctor, about whom he seemed very uneasy. "How do you keep the place staffed during this kind of weather?" Shigata asked the admissions clerk.

"Oh, we're on what's called storm crew," she answered. "The hospital sends all patients who can't be turned loose but who are stabilized enough to move to hospitals farther inland, to free up a lot of rooms, and then most of the personnel just move into the hospital. They put us on twelve-hour shifts, so there are always four or five nurses and at least one doctor on duty down here and enough other personnel available to keep the hospital running, and if they get too busy in any one area they just call up to the rooms and have some more people come down."

"That makes sense," Shigata said. That, basically, was what he'd done—he'd allowed unmarried officers with dependent children (that was only one woman, but he'd written it as a standing order for men or women) to take their families and head inland if they wanted to. All other officers, per a standing order issued by a police chief well before Shigata ever came to Galveston County, moved into the police station until the storm was over and things returned to normal.

"Oh, yeah, it works real well," the clerk continued. "Not to have to drive in that awful weather, and of course there's electricity and all here. My family boarded up the windows and drove up to visit some relatives in Tyler, and let me tell you, I am glad I didn't have to go. I mean, it's bound to be wall-to-wall people up there."

Suddenly, there was a tremendous crash outside. It wasn't thunder. Shigata, along with at least half the other occupants of the waiting area, headed for the door.

An ambulance, which had somehow managed to get through pounding rain and eighty-mile-an-hour winds to reach the hospital, had just struck the back of a new maroon and gray pickup truck that had been left at the ambulance dock. The truck's camper had toppled partway off, and the ambulance driver's door was jammed.

Dan Weston, who had followed Shigata outside while most of the others stayed at the door, stopped short and grabbed Shigata's arm. "That's my truck!"

"What?" Shigata said, turning to look at him.

"That's my truck! That pickup truck is mine. What the hell—" He vaulted off the dock, to reach inside the truck and grab for the keys. "How the hell did—"

Shigata grabbed him and dragged him back away from

the truck; even through this downpour he could see a small amount of smoke rising from the ambulance's engine. "Get that driver out," he ordered Weston, and ran himself to open the back door of the ambulance.

Two emergency medical technicians and a patient were inside; neither of the EMTs seemed more than shaken, and they were already attending to the patient themselves. Shigata ran back inside the building, forcing his way against the wind and rain. "Get me a fire extinguisher!" he shouted.

Someone handed him a foam extinguisher, and a couple of other people—including Richard Weston, who one could only hope was a better doctor than he was a patient—came outside to help Dan Weston with the driver, who was bleeding and unconscious from a head injury. Shigata, half-blinded by rain, sprayed foam on the engines of both vehicles.

The emergency-room doctor was outside giving orders to the people working to get the driver safely out of the front of the ambulance. Somebody had called for several orderlies, and they were pushing the truck out of the way so that other incoming ambulances would not be endangered. They'd move the ambulance as soon as the driver was out, and the Texas City Police Department could investigate the accident at their leisure, which wasn't likely to be very soon.

Richard Weston departed, presumably to return to his interrupted wait for head X rays. Shigata corralled Dan Weston.

"Let's find a quiet place to talk."

Dan Weston looked around. "You've got to be kidding."

"We can at least try."

The two men headed for the hospital cafeteria. The smells coming from it suggested that here was one place where food was available, hurricane or no hurricane, and without discussion Shigata opened the door, went in, got a tray and headed for the serving line.

The windows here weren't actually boarded up, just thoroughly taped over. Rain was pouring in where normally anybody would swear there weren't any cracks or gaps. Half the tables and chairs were sitting in puddles, and an enormous sign by the cash register warned that the floor was slick. Shigata led the way to a corner table that wasn't much wetter than the other tables.

"Now. Tell me how your truck happened to be out there."

Weston shook his head. "Damned if I know. You know I didn't drive it. I suppose Gwen must've."

"That makes sense," Shigata agreed, "except how did Gwen get it?"

"She knows the combination to my front door," Weston answered, "so it would have been easy enough for her to get in, and she knows where I keep the keys. If she couldn't get her car started and needed transportation, well, she knew I wouldn't mind—though I wish she hadn't left it—"

"Did you see her when she came in the door?" Shigata interrupted.

Weston nodded.

"You think she was up to parking the truck in the parking lot and walking in through that wind?"

"She couldn't have," Weston said. "There's no way. But she could have told me the truck was out there. I could have—"

"Weston, what was she talking about?" Shigata asked.

Weston shook his head. "Your guess is as good as mine. She was pretty incoherent."

"Was she incoherent?" Shigata asked, his eyes intent on Weston's. "Who killed them? Danny. Who wouldn't let her go? Danny."

"Now come off it," Weston said. "You know where I—"

"I know what you said," Shigata interrupted. "I know what you told me. But that's all I know. I don't know where you were last night. I don't know where you were this morning. The earliest knowledge I have of your location is when Quinn saw you, and at that time you were walking toward your brother's house from the direction of your condo."

"I told you what—"

"You told me, but should I believe it?"

Weston reached into his pocket and pulled out a keychain. "This is Gwen's key," he said. "She gave it to me. I don't know what your rules about search warrants and so forth are, but I guess in a hurricane things might be a little different. Hand me your notebook."

Shigata slid the notebook across the table, and Weston wrote four numbers. "That's the combination to my front door," he said. "It's a push-button lock. You need me to sign anything, I'll sign it. You go over there and see if there's any evidence I've been keeping Gwen—or anybody else—prisoner. But I'll tell you something, Shigata."

"What's that?"

"Gwen's not stupid. She's not hysterical. She's been drugged. I'm sure of that, from the look of her eyes, and I don't know how the hell she managed to drive over here. The shape she's in physically, I'd expect to find her on the side of the road somewhere. She was rambling like mad. She didn't mean I did any of those things she was talking about. But all the same, if she says she was held prisoner, then she was held prisoner. If she says somebody killed somebody, then somebody killed somebody. And she said 'them.' Somebody killed 'them.' So you're going to find several bodies, and my guess is they're going to be in her apartment."

"Why is that your guess?"

"Because I don't know what they—whoever they were—would be doing at my place. I left it locked and boarded up. Gwen knows the combination, so she could get in, but I sure don't see how anybody else could. My condo is a lot more secure than Richard's house. He's got all those nice deadbolt locks, but he's combined them with hollow-core doors and flimsy door frames. Whoever the builder on the condo was, he was security conscious. I have steel-core doors and steel door frames, and I program my lock myself so I can change it whenever I want to."

"Like whenever you change girlfriends?"

Weston chuckled. "Yeah. But I haven't changed lately. Gwen could move in with me any time she wants to. She hasn't wanted to, yet. If this doesn't change her mind, nothing is likely to."

"I heard you're divorced."

"You heard that from me."

"How come?"

Weston shrugged. "One too many pretty little interns. My wife's patience was not unlimited. So she took the kids and skedaddled. She's working for Kaiser-Permanente in Dallas now."

"She's a doctor too?"

"Yeah. We never should have married each other to start with. It was a lousy idea and a lousy marriage. But that's the way things work out." Weston stood up. "Are you through with me?"

"For now," Shigata said. "But you're going to have to either go with me or stay in the hospital."

"So what happens if you leave and then I leave?"

"You won't," Shigata said, very softly.

"How do you know I won't? My truck's drivable. All I'd have to do would be push the camper off—"

"Because in about two minutes I'm going to be on the telephone to the Texas City Police Department, and they're going to send an officer over here—as inconvenient as it will be to spare one at this time—and he's going to see to it that you don't."

"Oh. Well, I wasn't going to, anyway."

"Right," Shigata said, and neatly placed all his dishes back on the oddly shaped turquoise plastic tray. "You ready?"

"Yeah, I'm through." Without much show of grace, Weston took his tray over to the conveyor belt and set it down and followed Shigata out the door.

Richard Weston's gurney was gone. It turned out that he had already been X-rayed. He was standing in the hall of the X-ray area, looking at his own X rays. Dan immediately joined him.

"Damn," Dan said softly.

Richard, his tone extremely unhappy, said, "Yeah."

"No wonder you had a headache," Dan said. "We've got to get you on some antibiotics fast."

"I guess it's lucky I haven't felt like eating anything."

Shigata had a pretty good idea what they were both looking at, but just in case he didn't Dan traced it with his finger. "Depressed skull fracture," he said. "To you," he added.

There was a little splintering visible, and in the almost full-size X rays it was easy to see the curvature of what, if it wasn't a flashlight, was certainly shaped like a flashlight. The shape wasn't so evident on the clavicle, as the Westons—and presumably all other doctors—called what Shigata called the collarbone. The fracture was though.

There's no real way to put a splint or cast on a collarbone; the time he had broken his, all Shigata had was a sling and a sore collarbone for several weeks. So, presumably, Weston was going to have a sling for his fractured collarbone. The skull fracture was another matter.

"Is that going to require surgery?" Shigata asked.

Both Westons turned to look at him. "Obviously," Dan said.

"So you're not going to try to do it here?"

"I'm not going to try to do it myself, anyway," Dan Weston said, in a somewhat startled voice. "You think I'm crazy?"

"I guess a surgeon with a relative as the patient is like a cop with a relative the victim," Shigata said. "I speak from experience."

"Probably," Richard Weston said. "I mean, there are some things you just don't do. Not if you've got bat-ass sense." He was still intently studying the X ray. Shigata shrugged, walked into the X-ray office with his badge case open, and asked to use the phone.

"You want what?" the Texas City police dispatcher said two minutes later.

"I know it's a hell of a time," Shigata said, "but it's not my jurisdiction. I don't think he'll grow bunny feet, but I'd hate to risk it."

"I'll get you somebody over there," the dispatcher said, in a resigned tone of voice.

He made a second phone call, hoping the lines were still intact at Weston's house. Quinn answered.

"You still got the body there?" Shigata asked.

"No, we got it moved out. It ought to be over in the morgue now."

"You through with the crime scene?"

"Through enough that I can leave it if I get a patrolman over here to stand by."

Shigata gave him the address. "As soon as you're covered, drive over there—"

"Drive?" Quinn interrupted.

"Walk, then. I don't care. I should think it would be easier to drive. If a door's open, go on in. If it's not, wait for me outside."

"What do you think's over there?"

"More of the same," Shigata said, and Quinn whistled. "I don't know how long it'll be before I get there," Shigata added, "but if it is bodies, don't put it on the air. I don't want Southam back. Just say, 'That's affirmative,' or something like that."

"Gotcha."

Walking past the Westons, who were still studying X rays and now pointing things out to the emergency-room doctor who had joined them, Shigata braced himself to go back out into the wind and the rain to get his briefcase out of the car. He wasn't a large man, only five-eight and slender, and walking in this weather was more difficult for him than he'd have liked to admit. The briefcase retrieved, he went back into the hospital.

The papers inside were only slightly damp, which was better than he'd expected. Tearing the top two sheets off a pad of consent-to-search forms, he returned to the Westons. "Sign," he ordered Dan. "Unless you've changed your mind."

"I haven't changed my mind."

With that form signed and witnessed, Shigata filled out a second sheet and went looking for Gwen.

Her eyes were partly open, and she was talking about Danny. This time there was no doubt about what she was saying. "Danny wouldn't let me go. He made me take the Valium but I got away. I got away."

There was something wrong with that. She'd gotten away recently; she'd have gotten here sooner if she hadn't. Maybe Shigata didn't know where Dan Weston had been during the night or morning, but he knew where Dan Weston had been for the last five hours. If Gwen had taken enough Valium to have her in this condition now, she didn't take it five hours ago. She wouldn't have been able to drive a car much more than thirty minutes after she had taken it.

Which meant it wasn't Dan Weston—or, for that matter, Richard Weston—who gave her the Valium and whatever else was in her.

Now she was talking about phone calls. She didn't like the phone calls. Either she was telling Dan—Danny, she said—about the phone calls, or else Dan made the phone calls. Shigata couldn't tell.

"Gwen?" he asked. "Gwen? Can you hear me?"

"No, she can't hear you," a nurse interrupted angrily. "She is not conscious, and if she were she certainly wouldn't be up to talking with the police."

"Okay," Shigata said, and went back out into the waiting area.

What now? The courts had ruled that you have to have a search warrant, or a consent to search, to search a crime scene, but in this case, due to the storm, there was no way of getting a search warrant. The victim's condition precluded obtaining a consent to search. He couldn't risk waiting. There had to be a loophole.

There was. The courts had ruled that when the crime scene, or even the location of suspected contraband, is a vehicle that is likely to be removed from the jurisdiction before a search warrant can be obtained, it can be searched on probable cause alone. He had probable cause; surely nobody would dispute that. It was true that a house wasn't a vehicle, and a court case might come out of this, but he'd win if it did. An old frame house less than a quarter of a mile from the beach, during a hurricane—it wasn't likely to be driven away, but any reasonable person would say there was more than a slight possibility of its being blown away.

A patrolman came through the door, his yellow slicker dripping wet. The only way Shigata could tell what department he was from was by the fact that he was the same patrolman whom they had passed at a roadblock on their way to the hospital.

"Shigata?" he said. "Thanks for getting me indoors for a change." He shucked off the slicker; from the looks of his uniform, it was impossible to tell he'd been wearing a slicker at all.

"You're welcome. What's your name?"

"Lueders. Dave Lueders."

"Okay, Lueders, thanks for helping me out. You'll be indoors for a while."

"Hallelujah. Who'm I supposed to baby-sit?"

"This way."

The emergency-room doctor had gone. The Westons were still standing together looking at the X ray, apparently trying to determine the exact extent of damage and decide what to do about it.

"Gentlemen," Shigata said, and they both turned. "This is Officer Dave Lueders of the Texas City Police Department. Lueders, these are Doctor Richard Weston, who is presently suffering from a skull fracture and will probably be admitted to the hospital and put in a room in the next few minutes, and Doctor Dan Weston, who is not suffering from a skull fracture. Neither one of them has been charged with anything, but I don't want either one to leave the hospital."

"If you want me to watch 'em both, they're gonna have to stay together," Lueders pointed out.

"We'll stay together," Dan said, in a rather flat voice.

"Shigata, you didn't have to do this. I told you I wasn't really going anywhere."

"I didn't want you to be tempted. Look at it this way. You got Lueders in out of the rain. He's sure to be grateful."

Lueders grinned at the Westons. They did not smile back.

Gail was crying. The water that flooded Bayshore Road where the road ran under I-45 had continued to rise, and now water was foaming only a few feet below the top of the concrete where Melissa and Gail had taken refuge. Huge trees were knocking against it. If the concrete washed out, there was nowhere left to go. It was impossible to reach the service station now, not that it would have been any kind of haven if they could have reached it—they could see water washing over the door latches of the car.

Unconsciously, Melissa tightened her grip on her daughter. Gail, startled, turned just in time to see the car rock two or three times, turn slowly around, and begin to drift toward the break in the dike, where the storm-raised waters of Galveston Bay were washing through to mix with the hurricane water.

"Mommy?" Gail said tremulously. "What'll we do if—"

"It's all right," Melissa said. "It's all right, Gail. It's all right. It's all right."

But it wasn't all right. Melissa, cradling Gail's head so Gail couldn't see, watched numbly as another chunk of concrete broke out of one of the pylons and was carried away by the force of the waters.

THE MAN WHOSE NAME WAS DANNY, WHO WAS not Dan Weston, had been sitting lethargically for the last two hours. She was gone, there was no doubt about that. He'd searched all the places she might have hidden, even gone out in the storm to check that other place, but she wasn't anywhere.

She shouldn't have been able to get far. He'd found the window open, so she'd probably gone out the window. He should have left those boards over it. Then she couldn't have gone out that way.

But if he'd left those boards, he couldn't have watched the storm, couldn't have watched what he often couldn't see anyway but sometimes could—the black water boiling in the bay.

Probably she hadn't gotten far. Probably she was out somewhere in the storm. Probably she was dead. Perhaps she'd been blown into that boiling, foaming, churning, mad water. He was sure she was dead—but it wasn't the same. He should have killed her himself, the way he had killed the others.

The ways he'd killed the others.

He let himself smile at that.

He'd been practicing ways of killing people. How many different ways there are to kill people. He didn't have a gun—nobody would let him have a gun—but he didn't need a gun. Maybe it wouldn't be the same with a gun. There wouldn't be as much blood.

The knife she used for cutting bread.

The flashlight she used at night when it was dark.

The knife she used when she carved the roast.

The big black frying pan—

The cane she used to beat him when he was bad.

He let himself think about the woman under the bridge. The woman and the girl. They were bad. The girl was bad. She smiled at people she didn't even know.

The water would go down soon. The storm must be nearly over. Then he'd get to them.

Shigata fiddled with the dials on the radio, trying to raise the weather-service broadcast. He knew the broadcast frequency, but he wasn't picking up a transmission. Either they were off the air, or there was signal drift, or there was something wrong with his radio, which was very far from impossible.

The static suddenly cleared. "From the National Hurricane Center in Miami. Hurricane Anna, which suddenly reversed its path to move back out into the Gulf after its eye had come ashore, is now completely stationary. The eye of the storm is located less than one mile due east of the southeast corner of Scholes Airfield on Galveston Island. Water is washing over the Galveston seawall to flood low-lying portions of the Island, and the entire Texas City dike is under water. The Island is taking a severe beating from the landward side of the powerful storm, which is expected to resume motion sometime in the next two hours, with its probable second landfall somewhere in the West Bay area near Bayport or Texas City. The entire Galveston County area, from Lake Anahuac and San Jacinto Bay in the northern part of Galveston Bay to an area south of Chocolate Bay—

Shigata turned off the radio. He'd heard what he needed to hear. The storm wasn't going to swing north and let him do his work undisturbed. It wasn't going to let Melissa and Gail come home tomorrow or the next day.

He'd be lucky to make it to Gwen Hardesty's apartment. Once there, he'd better not count on leaving it anytime soon. The winds looked to be about sixty miles an hour right now, and gusting a lot higher. Making any kind of progress at all in this high-profile vehicle was next to impossible. It was taking his full concentration and the full strength of the engine to get anywhere.

It took his full concentration, but his full concentration wasn't on it. He was thinking about Melissa again. Thinking about Melissa, and wondering what he was going to do about the impasse their relationship, or nonrelationship, to be accurate, had been in, practically since the day they met.

A gust of wind came up and blew his car right off the road. He couldn't fight it because he'd let his speed pick up a little too much and he was hydroplaning. All thoughts of Melissa gone now, he fought to get the car under control before it rolled.

The car finally stopped and he got out to check on how he was going to get back onto the road. The wind knocked him over.

Flat on the road offering a little less wind resistance, Shigata wriggled back to the car. He opened the door. Clinging to it, he got back in, and managed, using both hands, to pull the door closed. He backed cautiously toward the middle of the road, and felt one wheel, then another, bump over the shoulder and back onto the road.

Congratulations, Shigata. You're back on the road. What do you do for an encore?

It was pitch-dark. They felt and heard, rather than saw, the water coming closer and closer. Garages, chicken coops, and piles of brush washed by, many of them taking deep gouges out of the concrete pilings. Melissa had quit saying "It's all right," because Gail wasn't stupid. She was old enough to know it wasn't all right.

This storm has got to stop sometime. It can't go on forever. But it doesn't have to go on forever for it to be forever for us. All it has to do is go on long enough for the flood to get about three feet higher, or bring down something big and knock it against this bridge. That's all it has to do.

Mark told me to leave two days before I did. Why didn't I do it? Why didn't I do it? Was I trying to commit suicide?

If I was, I shouldn't have tried to take Gail with me. She's not tired of living. She never knew Sam.

Sam is dead. That's no reason for me to want to be dead.

Oh, God, please take this storm away.

Shigata turned into the driveway of the old house. The driveway had all but washed out. Shigata parked next to Quinn's car and rolled down his window.

"How in hell did you get here?" Quinn shouted through his own open window.

"GOK," Shigata replied, hoping Quinn would know what that meant. Apparently he did, because he nodded.

"I haven't tried to go in yet," Quinn shouted. "Only been here about ten minutes myself."

"Who've you got at the Weston place?"

"Ames. Okay?"

"Looks like it's gotta be," Shigata shouted back. "Okay. Let's try to get inside."

Shigata got out of the car and was promptly blown over again. Quinn, shorter than Shigata but stockier, came to help him up. "You sure you don't want to just leave them bodies lay?" he shouted in Shigata's ear.

"Can't," Shigata returned.

"I know it."

It took both of them clinging together to get up to the relatively sheltered front veranda of the old house. The front door was standing open—no telling whether somebody had left it open or whether it had blown open. On entering, they found that this door led into a small entry hall, six inches deep in water. To the left was a long flight of stairs, the door at the top of which was closed. Directly ahead was another wooden door, also closed.

Weston had said Gwen's apartment was on the main floor. Shigata turned the knob. The door was unlocked. They walked in, overworked flashlights shining faintly through the pitch darkness.

Quinn gagged and then swore. After a minute, he asked, "You ever read *Helter Skelter?*"

"Yeah," Shigata said. "Yeah, I read *Helter Skelter*—and I can think of two ways we're better off than they were."

"I'd sure as hell like to hear 'em."

"We got rid of that son of a bitch Southam, so we don't have an assistant DA getting in our way. And it's just you and me, so we don't have a whole herd of excited rookies running around to mess things up and kick knives under the sofa and so forth."

"On the other hand, they didn't have a hurricane."

"That's true."

"And if we mess this one up, we've got nobody but ourselves to blame."

"Which means we better not mess it up."

"So how do you propose we work it? Look, Shigata, I'm serious. This house is liable to go any minute. We can't possibly get any help—Galveston can't spare anybody, and if they could nobody could get over the causeway. We're not equipped to work a complicated crime scene ourselves. We haven't got the equipment, we haven't got the time, we haven't even got any *light*. So what are we gonna do?"

"We are going to work this crime scene," Shigata said, "and we're going to do it as close to right as we can, given the circumstances."

"How?"

"Can you get out to my car and bring in the camera?" Shigata asked. "I've got flashlight batteries in my briefcase."

Quinn turned and looked out at the storm. He looked back at Shigata, and he looked out at the storm again. He headed for the door.

"Quinn."

"Yeah?"

"If you can't do it, say so."

"I can do it."

It took a few minutes for Quinn to get back in with the camera and a briefcase containing flashlight batteries, evidence tags, fingerprint powder and brushes, and assorted paraphernalia. In the meantime, Shigata had managed to locate a looseleaf notebook and a large pile of grocery bags. Propping his flashlight up for the needed light, he'd made a quick sketch of the layout of the apartment, and was now sitting on the living-room floor, enlarging the sketch and writing information below it.

Victim #1. White female identified by driver's license photo in handbag as Judith Grey. Lying on back on couch, head pointed approx. NE. Blond, blue, app. 5'4", 130 lbs. Wearing blue jeans, pink sleeveless sweater with metallic threads, no shoes. Throat cut almost to spine. L arm hanging over edge of couch above cocktail glass. L wrist slashed, blood ran into cocktail glass.

Victim #2. White female identified by driver's license photo in handbag as Josephine Martinez. Black, brown, app. 5'2", 135 lbs. Lying facedown on dining-room floor, head pointed almost due N. Wearing blue jeans, white T-shirt with BYU logo on back, blue sneakers. Black-handled butcher knife in back.

Victim #3. Unknown white female. Blond, blue, app. 5'7", 120 lbs. Lying on back in dry bathtub, head pointed NW, nude. Face and arms severely cut, unrecognizable.

Possessions in rooms indicate three women resident in apartment: Judith Grey, Josephine Martinez, Gwendolyn Hardesty. Fourth handbag in apartment living room belonging to W/F Terra Camacho. Third victim could be Terra Camacho but identification not possible without fingerprints.

Butcher knife lying beside overturned coffee table, substance on blade resembling blood. Paring knife lying on bathroom counter with substance on blade which appears to be blood.

"Why'd you just say 'appears to be'?" Quinn asked, looking over Shigata's shoulder. "It damn well is blood."

"You know it's blood and I know it's blood, but we're not scientists and we haven't run a test to be sure it's blood, so we can't say it's blood."

"That's stupid."

"That's not stupid, and somebody should have taught it to you a long time before now," Shigata returned. "One time I was tracking a wounded man through an alley. He'd gone through several hours earlier, so we knew we weren't going to catch him, but we had to find out where he'd gone. Every place he'd bled, I stopped and took samples. On my report I listed each sample as 'substance bearing the appearance of blood,' and I felt like a jackass doing it, because of course it was blood. But just in case, I took a sample of each one.

"I tracked him to the end of the alley, and there was no place he could have gone from there. I nearly went nuts over it. He could have caught a car at the curb about forty feet back, but there was this next puddle showing which way he was going. From there he just flat disappeared into thin air, as far as I could tell, until my samples got to the lab and the lab ran tests and found out that last puddle wasn't blood. It was brake fluid from somebody's car. The suspect had gotten into a car back on the road. My proof that he'd gone into the alley wasn't proof at all. So you don't call it blood, or brake fluid, or red toothpaste. Describe what it looks like to you, but let the lab decide what it is."

"But that *is* blood on those knives," Quinn argued.

"Probably. Almost certainly. But let the lab say so. Anything look funny to you?"

"Let me think about it."

Quinn walked slowly through the apartment, sweeping the place with his flashlight, and then returned to the living room, pausing on the way to sniff at a half-full pitcher of Margaritas on the dining-room table beside an overturned tequila bottle. "Yeah," he said. "Yeah. Something does look funny."

"What?"

"We're supposed to think there was a struggle. But there wasn't. He—somebody—threw that stuff in the living room around on purpose. That one on the couch and that one in the bathtub were both asleep when he got here."

"How do you know the one in the bathtub was asleep? We had a woman dead in a bathtub before and she really was killed in a struggle." There was nothing in Shigata's tone of voice to indicate that other woman had been his wife, and that he had been suspected for a time of killing her, but Quinn knew it.

"You can tell the difference between a real struggle and a faked one."

"How?"

Quinn looked around again and finally said, "Damned if I know how. You just can."

"That's right," Shigata said. "You just can. It's one of those things that comes of experience. Okay, was the one in the dining room asleep?"

"Hell, no. That one was trying to get away."

"So who was killed first?"

"No way to tell for sure. But if the other two were asleep, I'd think he'd go first for the one who was awake."

"Okay, how come she was awake and the other two were asleep?"

"Damned if I know."

"Say she was the one killed first. The other two slept through it. You're a sound sleeper. Think you could sleep through murder?"

"Dan Weston says he did."

"He was drunk, and Jean Weston was asleep. She almost certainly never woke up, so there wasn't any screaming. I figure that one on the dining-room floor did some screaming. So how come the other two didn't wake up? I mean, a bathtub isn't exactly the most comfortable place in the world to sleep."

"They were drugged?"

"How come they were drugged and the other one wasn't?" Quinn didn't say anything. Patiently, Shigata asked, "Did you notice her shirt?"

"Yeah."

"You know what BYU is?"

"It's that Mormon college—" Quinn stopped short. "Mormons don't drink. So if somebody drugged their booze, she wouldn't have drunk any of it."

"Good thinking."

"But you thought it all before I did."

"I've been trained to think that way. What are we going to do about it now?"

"Get a sample of the booze?"

"Right. Do we have any jars in the evidence kit?"

Quinn examined it. "Nope."

"Then next week we'll get some. In the meantime, go in the kitchen and look under the sink."

Trying for fingerprints was the tricky part. If the blood, which was everywhere, got onto areas where there might be fingerprints, it would cover and obliterate them. This meant that the knives had to be packaged in such a way that the bloody blades not only were lower than the handles, but would definitely stay that way while being driven back to the police station in a hurricane.

Sticky drinks cause the same problems. The glasses had to be carefully dumped out, with their contents preserved— Quinn had found a cache of empty, clean mayonnaise jars and their lids. The pitcher had to be treated the same way, and the lid on the tequila bottle had to be screwed down tight, so the few remaining drops couldn't escape.

All the trash cans had to be searched, in case something that might have contained possible drugs had been pitched into one of them. Usually thorough photographs had to be taken, in case the house really was knocked down when the storm came back onto land—and because in that case the bodies might be damaged or lost for good, each body had to be carefully fingerprinted for permanent identification.

Shigata asked Quinn to fingerprint the corpses. Quinn, gagging a lot, did it. Shigata ignored the gagging. If Quinn didn't want him to notice the gagging, then obviously he should not notice it. If Quinn did want him to notice it, then even more obviously he should not notice it. That was simple logic.

Normally, evidence would be taken to the car in an open cardboard box or in a large sack into which the smaller evidence sacks would be packed. It would be insanity to carry it out in that way in a hurricane. After some pondering, Shigata, feeling slightly guilty, took from under one of the women's beds a large suitcase. He packed the evidence in very carefully, so that none of it could shift as long as the suitcase wasn't turned on its edge in normal carrying position. In this wind, they couldn't risk carrying it to the car—it could be blown right out of their hands. He'd have to push it and crawl behind it.

"You think we're gonna be able to get out of here?" Quinn asked, looking at the packed suitcase Shigata brought into the living room.

"I don't know," Shigata returned. "Have a look outside and see what it's doing."

Quinn opened the front door, stepped through the little closed-in porch, and opened the second front door, just in time to see a huge mesquite tree wrench from the ground and roll toward the door as easily and lightly as a tumbleweed across the prairie. *"Shit!"* he shouted, and slammed the door and retreated. The old house shuddered on its foundations. "We're back in the wall clouds!"

"What was it?" Shigata asked, sitting hard on the floor just in time to keep from falling.

"You know that big ol' mesquite tree out in front?"

"Yeah."

"Well, it ain't there no more." Quinn sat down beside Shigata. Both men could feel the house rocking. "Shigata?"

"Yeah?"

"You know we may be fixin' to die?"

"The thought has crossed my mind. Why? You want to talk about it?"

"Not especially. Do you?"

"I don't see what good it would do."

"I don't guess there's much I've left undone that I could have done," Quinn said thoughtfully. "I mean, I wish I'd made more money, but I couldn't. Not honestly, and I wouldn't want it any other way."

Shigata chuckled. "I don't wish I'd made more money. I just wish I'd married Melissa."

"You've never even laid her, have you?" Quinn asked.

"Uh-uh."

"Why?"

Shigata turned to look at Quinn. "Would you have? You know what she went through with that bastard she was married to."

"So? She ain't married to him now."

"You know what I mean."

"Yeah. I know what you mean. But I wish I didn't. It sounds kinda rough on you."

"It is. But I guess it's rough on her, too. Quinn, I don't want to talk about it, okay?"

"Okay. Sorry. Wasn't trying to pry."

"I know you weren't. What the—"

At the same moment, Quinn yelled, *"Sheee-it!"* and dove for the back of the couch, dragging Shigata with him. By the time they stopped rolling the living room was full of glass, water, and approximately a third of the mesquite tree.

Quinn stumbled to his feet. "Where are you going?" Shigata yelled after him.

"To the bathroom."

"You know it won't flush—"

"Well, I'm sure as hell not going outside, and I don't want to do it in my pants!"

Quinn returned a few minutes later, the smell of fear strong on him. "You don't get the runs when you get scared?" he inquired.

"No, I wait till it's over with," Shigata answered. He stood up.

Quinn picked up the telephone, listened for a dial tone, shook his head, and put the phone down.

Shigata didn't ask Quinn who he wanted to call. Anybody who knew Al Quinn knew who he would want to call at a time like this. He wanted to call Nguyen. He'd married her twenty-two years ago in Vietnam, and he didn't love her one bit less now than he did then.

"Where are you going?" Quinn asked.

"To the bathroom."

"I couldn't flush."

"So what? I'm doing the same thing you did."

Quinn chuckled. "I thought you said you wait till it's over."

"It *is* over. That tree's not going anywhere else. Anyway, we couldn't both get in there at once."

When he got out of the bathroom he didn't return to the back of the couch. He shut the bathroom door firmly and stood in the hall, looking at the bedroom doors.

"Now what?" Quinn asked.

"Now I'm going to do something else that would normally be illegal. I'm going to start looking through papers and see what connections I can find between these women and either of the Westons. Of course, we know Gwen is Dan Weston's girlfriend, but beyond that—"

"Shigata, that really is illegal," Quinn said nervously. "And you never let me do stuff that's—"

"We've never been in a situation in which the crime scene was liable to be wiped clean off the map in the next three or four hours, either."

MARK SHIGATA WAS METHODICALLY TURN-
ing the papers, studying each one briefly by the glow of two
flashlights. Al Quinn, standing in the doorway watching
him, could see beads of sweat standing on Shigata's cheek-
bones and temples.

*I'm so scared I'm sick. He's as scared as I am, but he doesn't
stop. A fight is hot; not very many people get scared off a fight. Not
many of the kind of people that turn into cops, that is. I wouldn't
run off from a fight. But this is cold, sitting here waiting for the
building to come down over our heads. And he goes right on working.*

The house shook violently as something slammed into its
northeast side. The storm was coming in from the southeast,
whirling counterclockwise. Shigata jumped slightly, then
put the paper in his hand into a pile on one side of the desk
and went on turning papers.

"How do you do it?"

Shigata glanced up at Quinn and didn't pretend to misun-
derstand. "You just do, that's all," he said. "You just do.
You're doing it, too. If you couldn't handle it, you know
where the door is just as well as I do."

"I'm not doing anything, though. If you'll tell me what we're looking for I'll go check another room."

"I don't know what we're looking for. We're looking for anything that would show a connection with either of the Weston brothers."

"You've got a connection. Gwen Hardesty lives here. She was screwing around with Dan Weston."

"It wasn't Gwen who was killed," Shigata pointed out.

"That blond in the bathtub is her size and coloring. He might have thought he was killing Gwen and then found out later . . ."

"That's a possibility, but that's not the kind of connection I mean. I mean something that would have caused a single killer to—"

"That doesn't make sense."

"What doesn't make sense?"

"What do you think we're talking about?"

"We're talking," Shigata said, "about the fact that in the last two or so days, within a one-mile radius, four women have been murdered and one, at least apparently, held prisoner."

"And you think the same person did it."

"Yes," Shigata said. "Yes, I do."

"And you think there has to be some sort of connection between all the victims and the Westons?"

"I'm proceeding on that assumption. I might be wrong."

"I think you are wrong. Look, Shigata, why should there be a connection? I mean, you know as well as I do that serial killers usually use the same MO. So that suggests it's not even the same killer, and if it's not then why look for connections between the victims?"

"Usually," Shigata answered. "Usually serial killers use the same method all the time. But they don't always. So which is harder to believe, that a serial killer changed his weapon, or that just by mere coincidence, in the same night or at least the same weekend, somebody kills Richard Weston's wife, kills Dan Weston's mistress's roommates, and keeps Dan Weston's mistress hostage, apparently planning on killing her, too?"

"I don't like either story. There's always coincidence."

"I don't like coincidence."

"Synchronicity, then."

Shigata glanced at him. "I don't like synchronicity, either."

"Synchronicity happens."

"So does shit," Shigata answered. "I don't like either one. Okay, it's possible. Yeah, it's possible. But possible doesn't mean likely, and I don't think it's likely. Especially since all these girls living here seem to be interns, which makes another connection to—"

"Why would anybody *want* to kill one brother's wife and the other brother's girlfriend?" Quinn interrupted, ignoring Shigata's last sentence.

Shigata shrugged. "That, my friend, is what I'm looking for."

He went on looking through papers, while outside the rain died down to a sullen drizzle that stopped in a couple of minutes. For the third time that day, Galveston County was in the eye of Hurricane Anna.

"Anyway," Quinn asked, "if somebody held Gwen captive, where'd they do it?"

"Probably at Dan Weston's place. I haven't gotten over there yet, but . . ."

"Suppose nobody held Gwen captive? Suppose *Gwen* is the murderer?"

"Why would she be?"

"Gwen's sleeping with Dan Weston, right?"

"So he says. Look, you can't have it both ways. Gwen can't be the victim that got missed *and* the killer."

"I like this version better. Dan Weston admits he's not what you might call strictly monogamous, right?"

Shigata had quit turning papers over. His full attention was now on Quinn. "Just exactly what are you getting at?"

"Suppose Dan got Jean pregnant and Gwen found out."

"You sound like a soap opera. Did Dan get Jean pregnant? Will Gwen find out? Tune in tomorrow and find out—"

"Shigata, I'm serious. Suppose that did happen. Suppose on top of that Dan was balling the other girls and Gwen found out about all of it?"

"You're making Dan sound like a satyr and Gwen a psychopath."

"Dan admits he's pretty—uh—prolific, if that's the right word."

"It's not."

"Anyway, you know what I mean. And I never saw Gwen and you never saw her coherent so neither one of us knows shit about what she's like. But whoever killed Jean Weston—and whoever killed that girl in there in the bathtub—is not sane. Oh, legally, maybe. But not really, and you know it as well as I do."

"Do you think Dan was balling the girl in the BYU shirt?"

"She was human," Quinn said. "Or she could have just been in the wrong place at the wrong time. That happens, too." Then, hearing a familiar sound outside the boarded window, Quinn jumped violently. "Was that a shot?"

"It sure as hell was!" Shigata was already on his feet. "Shit, we're both stupid! We didn't even think about checking the other two apartments!"

The front door was jammed by the mesquite tree. They

went out the back door and down the stairs in the direction the shot seemed to have come from.

It wasn't quite a basement apartment—houses at sea level near beaches don't have basements. It was the ground floor, as opposed to the main floor, which in a house this near the water was going to be raised. The entryway was awash, and undoubtedly the apartment would be, too. "Nobody's in there," Quinn said. "They couldn't be. Not unless they're half duck."

"There's got to be somebody there. The shot came from—"

Another shot splintered right through the door to sing between Shigata and Quinn and slam into the wall behind them. "Son of a bitch!" Quinn yelled, flattening himself against the side wall as much as possible. "Open up in there!"

"Go away!" a woman yelled angrily from behind the door.

"Police!" Shigata shouted. "We're police officers!"

"Go away!"

"I'm Mark Shigata, chief of police. I've got Sergeant Quinn with me. I don't know who you want to shoot, but I don't think it's us."

Dead silence. Then the voice said, "Al Quinn?"

"Yeah," Quinn said.

"I used to know Al Quinn, when I was in high school."

"Then open the damn door. If you know me you know I'm harmless."

"But I don't know if you're really Al Quinn."

"Well, you ain't gonna find out if you don't open the door and look, now are you?"

The door opened a crack. Shigata, who was nearer it than Quinn was, could see a chain lock still firmly in place. "Let me see some identification," the woman said.

Shigata held out his hand wordlessly for Quinn's billfold. He placed it along with his own badge case in the woman's hand. The door promptly shut firmly, but a moment later was opened all the way. A gray-haired woman in hip boots was standing behind it, in a living room that was four inches deep in water and mud. Her face was as weathered as an old shrimp boat, and she was holding a .357 Magnum in one hand. The air smelled of cordite. "Come in," she said, handing the IDs back.

Shigata, looking in some dismay at the flood, asked, "Wouldn't it be better if you came out?"

She looked down at the water, shrugged, and splashed out into the entryway. She brought the pistol with her.

"Who were you shooting at?" Quinn asked.

"Somebody was tearing the boards off my bedroom window."

"Maybe it was the owner, thinking the storm was over," Shigata suggested.

She hooted at that. *"I'm* the owner. I rent out the main part of the house 'cause I don't need much room. And anybody that figures that there storm is over oughta stay in Kansas. Somebody was trying to pull the boards off my window. And he wasn't up to no good, neither."

"Are you sure it was a person?" Quinn asked. "There's a mesquite tree halfway through the main floor window—"

"Mesquite trees don't carry knives. I saw the knife."

"Let me get your name," Shigata interrupted. "I like to know who I'm talking with."

"Don't laugh," she said. "It's Carrie Nation."

"I'm sure you do great honor to the original," Shigata said.

"Not me," she retorted. "I like my bottle at night. Mama's bottle baby, that's me." She laughed loudly.

"I remember you now," Quinn said. "Your daddy used

to run a shrimp boat out of Jones Bay and you were always going out with him. Said you were gonna be a shrimper when you got out of school. But your name wasn't Carrie. It was Car."

"That's me."

"So how come you changed you name?"

"My daddy thought it was funny, naming me Car Nation. So I changed it soon as the old man died."

"Did you ever get your shrimp boat?"

" 'Course I did. You ever know me to say I was gonna do something and then not do it?"

"I never did. Not since you roped and tackled and hog-tied me into taking you to the junior prom."

She laughed. "Had fun, didn't you?"

"Yeah, but I never did learn to dance."

"That's all right, you had fun."

"Carrie, I got a wife and twelve kids. Them days are over and gone. How come you shot at the door if he was at the window?"

She glared at him. "Now, you know I'm not stupid. 'Course I shot at the window. Then right after that I heard you at the door, so I thought he'd come around. I think he's been upstairs—the girls left before the storm come in, but there's been somebody moving around up there. I couldn't call the police, 'course, with the phone out, and I couldn't leave 'cause of the storm, so I've just been down here deciding whether I ought to go up there or not."

"That was us moving around upstairs," Shigata said. "What made you think the girls left town?"

"They did leave town. Left their fridge open, I think, 'cause something up there smells like it died. Anyways, I can always hear them moving around, and these last three days I didn't—" She stopped suddenly. "They didn't leave town? They're up there?"

Shigata nodded.

"It's them I smell?"

" 'Fraid so," Quinn said.

"I thought it was rust," she said, suddenly looking frightened. "Them old pipes—I thought it was rust coming through the ceiling. I thought it was rust. Was it blood?"

"It was blood. Did you hear any kind of commotion up there? Maybe about the time the storm got here?"

Carrie scratched her chin with the gun barrel, a sight which made Shigata avert his eyes. "Not really. They play up there a lot—romp, dance, that kind of thing. I heard one of 'em running and kind of squealing a little, but that's nothing unusual. They've always got boyfriends over. One of them came to help 'em leave, in fact. That's partly why I was sure they was gone. He took stuff to the car a couple of times."

"When was this?"

"Friday night. About six-thirty or seven. He parked on the north side and I was boarding up windows on the south, so I didn't pay him no nevermind."

That was in the ballpark, in terms of time. Decomposition was pretty far advanced for death on Friday night, but when it is hot and wet it doesn't take long.

"What did he look like?" Shigata asked.

"I told you I didn't pay no nevermind. Just a kid. Young. I don't know. Twenty, twenty-five, somewheres in there. Are you a Jap?"

"Japanese-American."

Shigata was at least fifth generation in America, but that hadn't kept him from being born in an internment camp, where his mother was imprisoned while his father went off to fight World War II as part of the American forces in Europe.

He'd run into prejudice in expected places and, more frequently than he liked to remember, in unexpected places. This would be a tiresome time to cope with it.

"How'd you get to be chief of police in Bayport?" she demanded. "Last I heard that racist salamander Henry Samford was running the town."

Quinn chuckled. "Salamander?"

"I can't call him a snake in the grass," she said, " 'cause snakes ain't slimy. I think maybe salamanders are."

"Anyway, you're way the hell behind the times. Samford's dead. Been dead eight months."

"Ms. Nation," Shigata interposed, not wanting to talk about the cousin he had killed, his cousin who had been Melissa's husband and Gail's natural father. "Did you see what kind of a vehicle he was driving?"

"Who? The salamander? Anyway you s'posed to call me Carrie. Everybody does."

"Carrie. No, the boyfriend. The man who came over Friday night."

"It was a truck. Something small. Shortbed. Black, I think. He had it jacked up on great big balloon tires like a swamp buggy. About the stupidest damn thing I ever seen."

"I don't guess you noticed the license number?" Quinn asked.

"What would I be noticing a thing like that for?"

"Get it on the air," Shigata said. Quinn lifted the small radio out of its pouch on his belt and spoke into it.

The deep-maroon Datsun pickup, jacked up on Bridgeport tires, was parked in the garage behind the house Carrie Nation had converted into three apartments.

The garage was locked. There was no reason for anybody to look there. Carrie rented the garage out. It was not supposed to be occupied by a pickup truck, and she hadn't seen the truck driven into the garage. It was dark and rainy on Friday night, and she was busy. There was no reason for her to notice.

The car's owner was not in the garage, nor was he at his own home. He was back at Dan Weston's condo. He wasn't sure how much longer he was going to have it to himself, and he had some things to think about.

The plan was working out well enough, except for that one who got away. He'd have to take care of those two under the bridge, but that had to wait until the water went down. In the meantime, there were other things to do.

He could think better if he were doing something with his hands. It had always been that way. He remembered Her telling him, "If you just stay busy you can think a lot better."

So he went and got a steak knife and, methodically, began to rip the heavy gold draperies that hung at the broken window.

He'd read cop stories. He knew how cops worked. So far, everybody he'd killed was, in one way or another, connected with Them. He'd have to kill somebody else, somebody unconnected, so they'd think it was a crazy person doing it. He'd found that awful bull dyke in the basement, underneath where those women lived. She'd be a good one, and he'd tried to get in, but he should have known to leave her alone. She'd shot at him.

And hit him. Not much. Just a little.

Remembering that now, he looked, with mild surprise, at the trail of blood that led across the carpet, from the window where he'd pulled off the boards to enter, across the living room, down the hall, into the bedroom. *Got to do something about that.* He cut one of the strips of gold cloth into a narrower strip and tied it around his arm. That took care of the bleeding. It didn't really hurt much, and it didn't seem to interfere much with the way he used his arm.

He grew tired of ripping curtains. Anyway, how had he gotten from the living room into the bedroom? First, he was ripping the gold curtains in the living room across from the mirror, and then he was ripping the gold curtains in the bedroom, and he couldn't remember going from one to the other.

He went into the kitchenette and opened the refrigerator door. Not much in there. Maybe that was because he was a doctor. Maybe doctors didn't eat at home much. There were a few eggs in a cardboard carton. There was some milk. The milk smelled bad.

Danny got out the eggs and pitched them, one at a time, onto the sofa. That wasn't much fun. The sofa was already ruined from the rain that had poured in after the window broke. He took the remaining milk and poured it right in the middle of the bed.

Now, that was more fun. Symbolic, sort of.

Adultery.

That was why they had killed Her. Because of adultery. Not Her adultery—She wouldn't do a thing like that. Their own adultery. She was in the way, so they killed Her, and now he was avenging Her.

He couldn't let them catch him. Not yet. There were still a lot of people involved, a lot of people he had to decide what to do about. Some he would kill, some he would not kill—but he had to make sure they didn't find him, and that meant making it look like a crazy person did it.

So what do crazy people do?

Well, a crazy person who would kill some women would probably kill some more women. He would have to do that. Only, so many women had left town because of the storm. There were some black women and some Mexican women left in the projects, but he didn't want to kill them. None of it was their fault. He only wanted to kill the ones whose fault it was. He was sorry he had to kill that Mexican woman in that apartment, but of course she was one of Them, even if she was Mexican.

It was mostly blonds. Women with that whitey-blond hair.

Where was he going to find another blond woman to kill, in this kind of weather?

The storm had stopped again, but it would probably be back. The storm was doing all kinds of funny things, but for a while it was gone. He didn't want to try to drive the truck yet. It would be too easy to go off the road. If he got out and walked a little, there was that 7-Eleven up on the corner, if they hadn't closed it, or maybe they would open it because the storm had stopped.

After stopping long enough to urinate on the big-screen television set, he went out the front door.

The ground outside the window was thick with sticky mud, but it wasn't covered with water as the apartment was inside. The footprints weren't clear enough for an identification, so measured photographs wouldn't do a lot of good. They could see where he'd been standing, and a few splatters of blood.

"How the hell did he get here so fast?" Quinn wondered aloud. "It wasn't five minutes after the wind stopped before I heard that first shot. There ain't no way he got here through that wall of wind, *or* stayed outside during it."

"So what's within a five-minute walk of here?" Shigata asked Carrie.

"Nothing," she said succinctly.

"The upstairs apartment," he said. "Who lives there?"

"A fellow name of Ben Cummings. 'Bout my age. Lives

alone. And I *know* he was going inland because he told me so. And told me when he left, and gave me his key. I got it right here." She jiggled a key ring.

"Give," Quinn said, holding out his hand, and she dropped the key into it.

"The one with the red dealie on it."

"Okay."

Quinn departed, and Carrie commented, "This don't make sense."

"What doesn't make sense?" Shigata asked.

"That blood. If I'd hit him with a .357 he oughta still be here."

"You've got a point. Let's see if we can figure out what did happen." He began to trace with his hands along the one-by-twelves that had been nailed over the window.

Quinn came back. "Clean," he reported.

"Thanks. Now, look. Here's where the bullet came out through the wood, about two feet to the left of the footprints. So that's not what hit him. But look."

On the right edge of the bullet hole, a chunk of wood had broken out from the force of the shot. To the right, a few feet beyond the blood spatters and the footprints, was a large splinter, one end of it dark red with recent blood.

"That's what hit him," Shigata said.

"I better go get the camera," Quinn said.

"Good idea. Bring a few evidence bags, too."

"You sure she's not Gwen?" Carrie Nation asked, looking at the body in the bathtub without the slightest quiver of objection to the highly unpleasant odors that filled the room.

"Positive," Shigata said. "I saw Gwen alive this afternoon."

Carrie shook her head. "It sure looks like Gwen to me.

What I can see of it. 'Course, it's hard to tell who somebody is without their face."

Quinn left the bathroom hurriedly. Carrie, staring after him, demanded, "What's the matter with him? He took off like a bear was chasing him."

"I think he's got an upset stomach," Shigata said, trying hard not to smile.

"Oh," Carrie said. "Oh, well, I did notice somebody must've had the runs."

The woman pulled the car over to the side of the road. "Do you need some help?" she asked.

Danny started to say no, but then he took another look. Blond curls were spilling out from under the blue, billed cap. She was one of Them. That must be what she was doing out this way.

"Yeah," he said. "Yeah. I—uh—"

"Well, what's the problem?" she asked, rather impatiently.

"I—uh—" *What do I do now? How do I get at her?*

"You want to get in the car and tell me about it?"

"Yeah. Yeah, if that's okay with you. That'd be super."

She reached across to unlock the door for him, and he slid in beside her. "What happened to your arm?" she asked, looking at the improvised bandage.

"Oh—uh—one of the windows broke, and I guess some of the glass hit me." *The window did break, when the chair went through it. But that was a different time, and that wasn't what hit me. But she won't know. There's no way she can tell. I can tell her anything, and she won't know the difference.*

"You want me to take you to the emergency room?"

"No. No, it's not that bad. I just, uh, I was trying to get to a drugstore to get some gauze and stuff like that."

"None of the drugstores are open. I don't think any stores are open right now."

"Oh. You got—uh—have you got a first-aid kit or something like that?"

"No. Just Band-Aids, and you look like you need more than that."

"Why aren't you driving?" he asked suddenly. "Why are we just sitting here?"

She stared at him. "I'm not a taxi driver. Even if I was I'd have to know where you were going. Now, what can I do to help? Do you need to go to the hospital?"

He sat still. "Can I see your gun?" he asked finally.

"Certainly not. I never let anybody handle my pistol. Now, where do you live? Would you like a ride to your house?"

He didn't answer.

"What's your name?"

"I guess I don't need any help," he said. He began to fumble for the door handle.

"What's your name?" she repeated sharply.

He opened the door. She reached for him, but he slipped away and ran. She scrambled from the car to go after him, but she was a small woman. He was at least a foot taller, and he was running across a field where she couldn't possibly go after him in the car.

She reached for her radio microphone. Standing beside the car, watching him run, she said, "Car fourteen to headquarters."

"Stand by, car fourteen."

She watched him run away.

As soon as the rain stopped, Joey looked outside. *"Now* the storm's *really* gone," he said.

Steve, looking at the sky, nodded judiciously. "I think it is."

"Then let's go find Mommy. It isn't fair. She went to wash clothes. We know where she goes to wash clothes."

That sounded fair to Steve. It was true that their mother had told them to stay indoors, but that was a long time ago. Nearly a week, it felt like, and all the milk tasted bad and the cereal was gone and they couldn't make peanut butter sandwiches because the bread had this funny green stuff on it.

It wasn't far, only two blocks away. They walked those two blocks and there was the car, the twelve-year-old Dodge Dart their mother had driven as long as the boys could remember.

The door of the laundromat wouldn't open. There were boards over all the windows, but Steve hoisted Joey up so Joey could look through a crack in the boards.

The patrol car, coming by minutes later, found two small boys crying hysterically. Mommy was asleep on the floor inside the laundromat. And her head was all funny like on *Friday the Thirteenth*.

The patrolman didn't need to be hoisted up to look through the crack. What he saw wasn't pleasant.

He was on the radio describing it when the policewoman tried to break in with her report.

"**I** CAN'T TELL THE CHIEF," THE DISPATCHER said, " 'cause the chief's ten-six with his radio off."

"Then use the land line," the patrolman said impatiently.

"Oh, sure, and next thing I'll do, I'll fly to the moon. Unaided."

"Well, what am I supposed to do? I've got these little kids out here, and I already told you about their mom—"

"I don't know what you're supposed to do," the dispatcher said desperately. She'd been a dispatcher only ten weeks; the patrolman had been a patrolman only twelve weeks.

When Mark Shigata took over as chief of police, the department—normally twenty officers and four dispatchers—was down to eleven officers and two dispatchers. He'd hired, and he'd arranged for training, but he'd made up his mind he wasn't going to hire anybody unfit just for the sake of filling vacant slots with warm bodies. The department was up to strength now, but with the exception of Mark Shigata and Al Quinn, it was a department of rookies. There wasn't one patrol officer or dispatcher with more than a full year of experience.

"I'll keep trying to raise the chief, and I'll try to get an ME's investigator over there. I don't know what else to do."

"What about these kids? Can't you get somebody from Welfare to come get them?"

"You know I can't reach Welfare, it's on the Island. If I could, I doubt there would be anybody there. If there was anybody there—"

"Never mind, never mind," the patrolman said, suddenly remembering that this less-than-edifying conversation was going out over the airwaves. "I'll stand by. But keep trying to get the chief."

"And you're sure of that?" Shigata asked.

They were sitting in one of the bedrooms of the main floor apartment—Gwen's, apparently. It was out of water and farthest from the bodies and the exceedingly malodorous bathroom. Somebody was supposed to be en route to pick up the bodies and transfer them to the morgue, but Shigata had been told not to expect anyone for at least thirty minutes. And if no one got there in the next thirty minutes then most likely no one would get there for the next four to six hours.

Carrie nodded emphatically. "Posilutely. All three of 'em were interns and all three of 'em were working with Dan Weston in some sort of research project. I always thought it was kind of funny, myself, because they'd be romping up here like little kids, you know, jumping around and popping each other with towels, and next thing you knew they'd be settling down talking. I couldn't understand a word they would say.

"But they was nice girls. Real nice. You asked about 'em smoking. No. None of 'em smoked. They wouldn't let nobody in the place that smoked—that's why that cigarette butt you found in the kitchen was so funny. But that's not what I meant by nice girls. I mean they was real nice. Caring. Like that. Look at me. I know what I am. I'm an old battle-ax. It's been a hell of a long time since I was Daddy's carnation, but they never said so. They treated me nice. They never made me feel—grotesque."

"You ain't grotesque, Carrie," Quinn said. "You just got character."

She laughed. "I ain't *got* character, I *am* a character."

"I appreciate the information," Shigata said. "You've made a lot of things much clearer than they were."

"You gonna get him?"

Shigata nodded. "I hope so, Carrie." He picked up Quinn's radio. "Car one, ten-eight."

Under the circumstances, that was a joke. Ten-eight means in service, ready to answer calls. He might answer a call from here and he might or might not get to wherever the call was, depending on how close it was and how bad the roads were and how soon the storm closed back in. He figured there were maybe twenty minutes left before the winds, now almost calm, topped a hundred and fifty miles an hour again.

"Car one, I've been trying to raise you." Dispatcher Eve Booth, who had celebrated her twenty-second birthday the previous week, sounded very upset. "We've got another homicide."

Shigata almost swore on the air. "Where? What kind?"

"Judson's Laundromat. A woman, stabbed and cut up. Barlow said it looks like she's been dead two or three days."

"That's just three blocks from the police station. Why was she just now found?"

"The building was boarded up, so nobody looked inside. Her sons walked down there and found her. Chief, they're little kids, eight and ten years old. We can't get hold of Welfare. What should we do with the kids? Barlow said to ask you."

"Stand by," Shigata said. He turned to Quinn. "Would Nguyen—"

"Get 'em over there," Quinn said quickly. "Sure. She'll always take on more kids."

"We got an officer on the scene?" Shigata asked.

"Ten-four. Barlow. He's staying outside, though. Nobody's gone inside yet. Barlow figured to wait for you."

Eve was trying very hard to sound just like somebody on a cop show on TV. She wasn't succeeding very well.

"Good. Tell Barlow to stand by. I'll be en route. If anybody from the ME's office or the DA's office gets there before I do, Barlow's not to let them in. Pull all the authority he has to, but keep 'em out. Clear?"

"Ten-four."

"I'm en route." Shigata put the radio on the table. "Can you stay here?" he asked Quinn. "I need to head over there, and I'm not ready to release this scene yet."

"Yeah."

"I don't know how much more this building's going to take. If you think it's about to go, get out. Carrie, you go with him if he decides to leave. I don't want you here by yourself."

"This is my place," Carrie objected. "What are you doing giving me orders? You declaring martial law or something?"

"No, but I've got more than enough corpses. Don't set yourself up to provide me any more. Bear in mind, whoever did this could come back."

"Yeah, but I got a gun."

"I don't want *any* more corpses."

"What about them?" Carrie asked, gesturing toward the

front of the apartment. "I mean, if the building comes down, they'll just—be left here."

"They're already dead," Shigata said. "Nothing can happen to them that hasn't already."

He didn't know how much longer the calm would hold. Not much longer, certainly. He was taking a chance, getting out on the road this close to the return of the wall clouds, but he'd driven enough today that now, in the dark, he had a pretty fair idea which streets to drive on and which streets to avoid, where he could speed up and where he had to slow down.

It was completely dark by the time he reached the laundromat, darker than it ever was on a normal night. There were no streetlights, no ambient light from houses and store windows and neon signs—just headlights. His own, and the headlights of Barlow's patrol car. And the headlights of Joel Moran's car, which was fine, and Jason Southam's car, which wasn't so fine.

Shigata didn't recognize Southam's car, but he did recognize Southam, standing at the door of the laundromat with Barlow and Moran blocking him and two very dirty small boys, barefoot in shorts and T-shirts, watching excitedly. Shigata got out of the car and all three men and both small boys headed for him.

"These officious—," began Southam.

"This civilian—," began Barlow.

"This moron—," began Moran.

"Shut up!" Shigata yelled.

All three continued talking in a completely incoherent medley.

"I said shut up!"

Silence.

Wind could be heard in the distance. Another patrol car pulled up, and Officer Claire Barndt got out, trying as usual when around the chief to hide her long blond hair under her cap.

Shigata had never mentioned her hair to her; and took her trying to hide it as a sign of a guilty conscience. *After this storm is over I've got to have a word with her about a haircut. They think it's a matter of looks. They don't realize it's a matter of safety.* He had to be tired, he thought, for his mind to be wandering with all this going on. But for a moment he had a sudden, vivid, flash of memory, something he'd seen years ago in a police department in Georgia. There was a new policewoman there who was taking full advantage of the fact that the department had established no haircut code for women; she was ignoring the fact that every other police-woman on the department either had short hair or kept her long hair pinned up when she was on duty. Until one day, as Shigata was coming out of the records section with some information he'd gone to pick up, he saw four other police-women surround that woman in the hall. All were talking to her very quietly; judging from the expression on her face, she didn't seem to be paying much attention. And then, without any warning Shigata ever saw, one of the women grabbed the mane of long hair and yanked. The victim yelped, nearly fell, and someone—Shigata couldn't tell if it was the woman who'd yanked, or one of the others, said, in a very cold voice, "If I'd been a prisoner I'd have broken your neck. Now go get your fucking hair cut or else pin it up off your neck."

The next time Shigata saw the woman, her hair was properly off her neck.

There were no experienced policewomen here to give Claire Barndt the same advice. So Shigata was going to have to tell her the story. And then see whether she would take the hint, or whether he would have to put it out as an official policy.

Claire Barndt had very pretty hair. But that wasn't the point.

Claire walked over to Shigata's car. "Dispatch said you needed me over here."

"I do?"

"It was me that needed you," Barlow said hastily.

"What for?"

"To take care of these kids."

"I'm not a baby-sitter. Anyhow, I need to tell the chief—"

"Barndt," Shigata said, in a carefully controlled voice, "I agree that you're not a baby-sitter. But I believe that you are aware of what is inside this building. We don't need these children here. I've made arrangements for them, but there isn't time to get them there before the storm closes back down. So take them to the police station, wash their faces, feed them, and stay with them until the roads are passable again. You're not going to be driving for about an hour, anyway."

"Yes sir, but I need to tell you—"

"Tell me later."

"But—"

"Tell me later," Shigata repeated.

She shrugged. "Okay," she said, and turned to the children, saying something under her breath that sounded very much like "You'll be sorry." Then, more loudly, she said, "What're your names, fellows?"

"I'm Steve Jester," said the larger boy. "This is Joey. He's my brother. Our mom's in there. She's asleep and they won't let us go in and wake her up."

"She might be real hard to wake up right now," Claire said. "Where's your dad?"

"We haven't got a daddy," Joey said.

" 'Course we do," Steve retored. "Everybody has a daddy. Mommy said so. But ours doesn't live here."

"Know where he does live?"

"Uh-uh. We're gonna get a new dad, anyway."

"Oh," Claire said. "Well, let's—"

"Wait a minute," Shigata said. He knelt on the wet pavement to look into Steve's face. "You're going to get a new daddy?"

"Uh-huh. Mommy said."

"Do you know his name?"

"Sure. His name is Ben, and he's real nice."

"Where does Ben live?"

"I don't know."

"Does Ben smoke?"

"Smoke?" Joey asked doubtfully.

"You know, silly!" Steve said. "Smoke cigarettes. Uh-uh. Ben doesn't smoke."

"What kind of work does Ben do?"

"I don't know. He drives a car."

"What kind of car?"

"A blue car."

"Do you know Ben's last name?"

"Uh-uh," Steve said. "Is that a real gun?" he asked Claire.

"Yeah, it's real."

"Can I see it?"

"No, I don't let people handle my gun."

"I guess that's all," Shigata said. *You look at the husband first. If there isn't a husband, you look at the boyfriend first. This time—Oh, hell.* "Fellows, this is Officer Claire Barndt, and she's going to get you a sandwich."

"We're not supposed to take food from strangers," Steve said.

"But we're police," Claire said. "That makes it okay. Come on, we want to get where the sandwiches are before the storm comes back."

"You mean it's coming back *again?*" Joey wailed. "Steve said it was really gone this time!"

"Maybe it'll be really gone by tomorrow."

"Now," Shigata said, after Claire had departed with the children, "we are going to go into the laundromat. But I'm laying down some ground rules first."

Southam bristled. "What right have you got to give me orders?"

"I thought we established that this morning," Shigata said. "But in case we didn't I'll go over it again. I am the chief of the Bayport Police Department. I am a fully qualified member of the bar. I am the officer in charge of this investigation. I am in charge of determining who committed the crime. You are on the prosecutor's staff. You have partial responsibility for prosecuting the case in a court of law—but only *after* I have developed a suspect and established sufficient probable cause for an arrest warrant. Now, we have an agreement with the district attorney's office that allows a representative from that office to be present during the investigation of what is potentially a capital felony. I very much doubt that you are the person that office would send if your boss had a choice, but as you are the only person presently available, I'm allowing you to stay. But you're on probation, so to speak—cause trouble and, as I said this morning, I'll throw you out. Got me?"

Southam didn't answer.

"Moran knows what he's doing at a crime scene," Shigata continued. "Barlow, you've had training but no practical experience to amount to anything. Southam, you have no official responsibility here, except that of an observer. So when we go in, I want anybody who might feel tempted to start touching things to walk around with his hands clasped behind his back. Nothing—I repeat, *nothing*—is to be moved before it has been photographed and before I have made an appropriate sketch and taken measurements. Is that clear?''

"Yes sir," Barlow said.

"Sure," Moran said.

Southam still didn't say anything.

"That woman's been dead since sometime Saturday afternoon," Shigata said. "We know because Quinn checked buildings late Saturday afternoon to see which ones were boarded up, and this one was locked and boarded up at that time. I saw it open at two."

"I thought—" Barlow began, and then stopped.

"You thought what, Barlow?"

"She looks to me like she's been dead three or four days. I mean, her face is green, and all those fluids—"

"Decomposition is fast in a hot, wet climate. You're right. Under normal conditions, it would take a body three or four days to reach the state that one is in now. Which means, by the way, that the air in there is going to stink worse than you can possibly imagine if you've never smelled it before. If you have to get sick, go outside to do it.''

"I've got some Lysol spray in the car," Moran said.

"All that'll do is make you hate Lysol spray," Shigata answered. "At least it's never done any good for me. Has it for you? You can use it if you want to."

"Doesn't do me any good, either," Moran said. "I've just got it there because some people think it helps. I've also got a floater mask, but that never helped me any either."

"What's a floater mask?" Barlow asked.

"It's sort of like a cheap gas mask," Shigata answered. "Theoretically, it filters out bad odors. They've never helped me noticeably."

"Why do they call it a floater mask?"

"Because the worst-smelling corpses tend to be the ones that have been in water a few days."

"So does anybody want to borrow mine?" Moran asked. "I won't be using it."

"I guess not," Barlow answered.

Southam, not to be outdone, also declined.

"If necessary, we'll break the glass out of the door. I don't think that will be necessary; I think I can get the lock undone."

"Well, you better do it fast," Moran said. "The stars to the southwest are gone. That means we got about five minutes."

Shigata turned and started to work.

The police car was still there, Danny saw. There'd been a police car there for a couple of hours—two of them, most of the time. Maybe he could get in and get the truck without the police seeing him and maybe he couldn't, but he did know that he didn't want to take the risk.

It was all that damn bull dyke's fault. She was the one who had called the police. She had to be. Otherwise, nobody would have found them until after the storm was over.

He'd seen the stars blotted out, as the wall cloud moved closer. Well, he couldn't get the truck. He would need it to get to that woman, but he'd sat through hurricanes before. It would be tomorrow morning before the water under the bridge had gone down enough for him to reach her. He could get the truck sometime during the night. The cops would be gone by then. They couldn't leave now, of course, but when the wind died down—

He had to get to cover *now*. The wind was so near he could hear it. That meant there was only one place to go. The place he didn't want to go.

Major annoyances, minor annoyances. He didn't know

which one to call being out of cigarettes. At least he could get some cigarettes there. He'd have to be fast, but he'd have to be quiet, too.

Melissa, too, had seen the stars blotted out by the approach of the wall clouds. Gail was asleep this time, a soft warm bundle in her arms, both of them inside the hollow space Melissa had located inside the concrete structure. With any kind of luck, Gail would sleep through this one. This should be the last—Melissa couldn't remember any storm reversing like this more than once.

By sometime tomorrow the water should be down, somebody should be able to get them out. At least somebody knew they were here—that young man she'd seen earlier in the day. He hadn't been back, but he couldn't come back. Anyhow, it wouldn't have done any good if he had. There wasn't anything he could do.

I want to go home.

How long had it been since she'd thought that? Had she ever thought that before?

Home when she was a kid was a nightmare. Something to forget, not to remember as other people remembered their childhood homes. Three girls living together, the middle one a half sister to each of the other two by a different parent, the oldest and youngest not related to each other at all. And the old man raping all three of them first and then running them like a herd of cattle, running them into bars, putting them out on the street, so that when he finally died none of them knew any way to live except on the street.

Then she married Sam, and that was supposed to be wonderful because Sam was rich, Sam would give her all the money she wanted, and he had. Given her money—and given her hell, until the only thing that stopped her from killing herself was the thought of Gail, because her sister

Wendy was taking care of Gail so Sam would never know, so Sam couldn't kill Gail as he had killed Lucie. But her sister wouldn't keep Gail if Melissa couldn't pay. So Melissa had stayed alive so she could keep paying her sister to keep Gail.

I didn't know my sister had married Mark Shigata. But if I had known, it wouldn't have made any difference because I didn't know Mark. I would have thought he would be just like the old man, just like Sam, because I didn't have anything else to go by.

I didn't know home could be a quiet place, where nobody hurt anybody, where nobody went around trying to find big ways and little ways to come out ahead of everybody else. A place where I could read and grow flowers.

I didn't know there was a man who would make jokes that didn't hurt anybody. Who would say "please" and "thank you" and look at me and smile.

Now I want to go home. I want to go home. I want this storm to stop so I can go home.

The lock clicked and snapped. Shigata pushed the door open and turned his head away from the stench that poured out of the room. Then, resolutely, he entered. Barlow dutifully held a flashlight to give Shigata a view of the scene. Shigata began taking notes on what he saw.

Victim is white female, approximately 5'3", about 130 lbs. Blond hair about shoulder length, eyes blue. Victim is lying on back with head pointed approximately east-northeast. Right arm is at side, left arm is raised. Defense cuts on both hands.

So, she'd fought. Unlike the girl in the BYU shirt, who'd only run, this woman fought. But it didn't do her any good. *Victim is wearing blue denim jeans, an embroidered blue chambray shirt, blue plastic thong sandals.*

He looked around and continued writing.

An overturned laundry basket is lying approximately four inches due west of victim's left hand. A handbag presumably belonging to victim is lying on sorting table approximately eighteen inches northwest of victim's head.

He continued walking, looking, pausing to write. *Trash can north of west sorting table is empty. Trash can north of east sorting table contains one empty Camel cigarette package.*

He knelt and examined the body without touching it.

Victim's face and arms have been cut repeatedly. All this appears to be slashing; there is no evidence of stabbing. A cigarette butt, make cannot be determined at this time, is lying under victim's left ear.

Moran was taking photographs.

"Moran?"

"Yeah?"

"Can we have copies of your pictures, so I don't have to take any?"

"Sure. Can I have copies of your sketch and so forth?"

"You bet."

"You want me to do anything?" Barlow asked.

"Not yet," Shigata said. "I'll have something for you to do in just a minute."

Suddenly, the winds raged, louder than a thousand trains, and the front door they'd left open slammed shut so hard the glass shattered and streamed in fragments toward them. Everything, including the investigators and the victim, was blown toward the wall at the back of the laundromat.

Shigata grabbed the handbag as it flew through the air and fought his way to the area behind the washers, which he knew, having used them himself a time or two, were bolted to the concrete floor. He didn't try to shout at the others to come with him; they wouldn't have heard, and in any event if they weren't smart enough to think of this for themselves they shouldn't be out of diapers, much less into law enforcement. He handed the bag to Moran, because if he laid it down even behind the washers it would certainly be blown away, and dove back out again to grab for the east trash can.

"What do you want that for?" Barlow shouted in Shigata's ear when he got back to relative safety.

"It's got the cigarette package in it."

"What the hell do you want a cigarette package for?"

"Fingerprints," Shigata yelled.

Which, of course, meant he couldn't get the cigarette package out of the trash can without tweezers, because if he did he'd leave his own fingerprints on it, and he couldn't let it blow away. That was a little awkward.

You've got a problem, Shigata. Now what are you going to do about it? A cigarette package is about the hardest thing in the world to get prints off of at the best of times. Just about anything rubs the prints out. You can't use regular fingerprint powder, or even mag powder, because they'll rub the print out. The best thing to use is powdered Xerox toner.

But anything that delicate can't be picked up with just anything. You can't pick it up with a paper towel or a handkerchief, assuming you happened to have a paper towel or a handkerchief, because that would rub the prints out. So what are you going to do about it?

Lead, follow, or get out of the way.

He'd brought the evidence-collection kit inside. There were tweezers in the kit. The problem was getting the kit, collecting the cigarette package without rubbing it against anything, and finding something to put the cigarette package in once he had collected it. The rest of the problem was that he didn't have very long to think about the problem, because if he didn't collect the package soon, it was going to either blow away or become drenched.

So he'd better think very, very fast. Or lose the evidence,

to say nothing of looking like an ass in front of three people to whom he had presented himself as an expert.

He sat on the floor with his back to a washing machine, holding the trash can in front of him to protect it as much as possible, thinking as fast as he possibly could.

"Al?" Carrie called.

"What." Quinn was methodically searching through the papers. Like Shigata, he hadn't the slightest idea what he was looking for, but he figured he'd know when—if—he found it.

"This kitchen is furnished, you know."

"What does that mean?"

"It means I buy all the pans and dishes and knives and stuff like that."

"Okay."

"So I've been checking, and there's something missing you need to know about."

"What's that?"

"A meat cleaver." If Quinn had known that the meat cleaver and the man who took it were almost directly above his head at that moment, he would have been able to handle the situation.

But he didn't know it.

Danny was lying on the floor listening to the conversation below. He'd been wrong about the cigarettes—there weren't any here—but at least he was out of the wind. And the conversation below was interesting.

They weren't on to him. He was sure of that now, from what they were saying.

They couldn't sit in a row. The double row of washing machines was at a ninety-degree angle to the front and back walls, parallel to the side walls, so they had the depth of five machines to protect them, but the width of only two.

They were sitting in a small circle that would have been smaller and better protected from the wind and the rain and the glass that was still flying everywhere if the circle hadn't also included one very large trash can containing one empty cigarette package.

"What've you got that trash can for?" demanded Southam for the third time.

"I already told you."

"You don't need the trash can. You just need the cigarette package."

"Right. But I have to get it right or—"

Southam reached for the cigarette package. Shigata, holding the trash can, couldn't turn it loose fast enough. Barlow and Moran reached for Southam, but neither one of them could get him before he got the cigarette package and held it up triumphantly.

Shigata punched him in the face.

It felt great.

To Shigata.

At that moment Barlow's radio, which had been turned up to full volume in the hope that somebody could hear it over the storm, squawked, "Headquarters to car one!"

Shigata nodded, and Barlow said. "Go ahead for car one."

"Officer Lueders from Texas City called and said Dan Weston wants to see you."

Shigata reached over for the radio, and Barlow handed it to him. "Right now?" he asked wryly.

"Well, when you can."

"Ten-four." Shigata glanced over at Southam, who was sitting with his back to the back wall, nursing his jaw. "Keep your hands to yourself at a crime scene."

"That's a felony!"

"What's a felony?"

"You just hit me for no reason at all—" Southam's voice trailed to a halt. Barlow and Moran were laughing.

"You're a jackass," Shigata said. "By all means take a warrant if you feel like it. But keep your hands to yourself at my crime scene from now on."

The flashlight batteries had run down completely. There was no way to do anything. Quinn and Carrie were sitting side by side on the floor of Gwen's bedroom.

"How come you never did get married?" Quinn asked. "I know it's none of my business, but—"

"Rex got killed," she said. "You remember when Rex got killed?"

"I remember," Quinn said. "I was there. Him and me enlisted together, went through boot camp together—went to Nam together."

"Oh yeah, I forgot. Well, he got killed. He got killed, that's all. And I didn't want to marry nobody else. He left me his GI insurance. That's what I bought the shrimp boat with. We was gonna run that shrimp boat together when he got back." She was silent for a moment. "Things don't always work out the way you plan."

"No. No, they don't, do they."

Danny rolled over on his back.

Things don't always work out the way you plan.

That was for ordinary people. Not for him.

Things would work out right for him.

That woman under the bridge—

PUSHED BY THE WIND, WHICH, SHIGATA SUS-pected, wasn't far off two hundred miles an hour, the body was slowly, inexorably, sliding toward the back of the laundromat where the men had taken refuge. It was like something out of a horror movie, sitting in the lee of the washers watching the body move over the rain-soaked, glass-covered floor.

Sooner or later it would slide into something that would stop it—the big extractor washers, perhaps, or the space between the office and the storeroom doors. Probably the latter. The wind was blowing obliquely from the southwest through the shattered door, and it was coming in a counterclockwise movement, so everything was being blown in a vaguely northeast direction, to the northeast corner where the office was, with the storeroom directly across from it built into the back wall of the laundromat.

Suddenly, irrationally, Shigata felt very nervous about the closed door with the red and yellow office sign on it, the closed door that led out of the building, the closed door with the rest-room sign on it, and the closed door that was unmarked but which he knew led to a storage room, where small, dispenser-size boxes of detergent and bleach and fabric softener, plastic bags, and washer parts were stored.

What was behind those doors? *Who* was behind those doors?

Almost certainly, nothing, nobody at all. Nobody would have stayed here.

But what could the killer have left here?

The urge to get up, to force his way through the wind and open those doors and look behind them, was powerful. He sat still, resisting it, because he wan't Superman and even if those doors were unlocked and an avatar of Jack the Ripper was hiding behind every one, Mark Shigata wasn't strong enough even to reach them, much less to open them right now, in this wind.

"Somebody's moving around upstairs," Carrie said.

"There can't be," Quinn said. "I checked it. Remember?"

"Just 'cause there was nobody there when you checked don't mean nobody's there now."

"Through this—"

"They could have got in before it started."

"Then we'd have heard them sooner than this."

"Not necessarily."

Quinn shrugged. "Okay." He stood up.

"Where are you going?"

"To check."

"Not without me!"

"You don't have any business—"

"Just 'cause I'm a woman—"

Quinn sighed and turned toward Carrie's voice. "That's not why at all. I'd rather have you as a backup than three-quarters of the men I know. But you're a civilian. I'm a cop.

It's my job. Your job is shrimp fishing. I don't have the legal or moral right to take you—"

"Just 'cause women can't be cops—"

"Carrie, don't you *ever* pay any attention to the news?"

"Not since Goldwater didn't get elected."

"That was a long time ago. We got twenty sworn officers. Five of 'em are women."

"Oh. Since when?"

"Since Shigata got to be chief of police. Four of 'em, anyway."

"I knew there was some reason why I liked that man."

"Now are you gonna let me go upstairs and check?"

"How are you gonna check when you can't see nothing?"

"Damned if I know, Carrie. Listen for his breathing, I suppose."

"What if he hears yours first?"

"Then I guess we got problems."

"Why don't you just stay here instead?"

"Because I think you may be right."

He didn't just think it. He was almost certain he had heard someone walking up there.

He felt his way across the room, braced himself against the stench that would be far stronger when he opened the door, cursed the queasy stomach that complicated his life as a cop, and headed out into the hall, trying to remember what walls and what furniture were where. He didn't want to stumble over the body that still lay on the dining-room floor, still with the knife in its back that ideally would be removed only by the pathologist.

He didn't stumble over the body. He didn't get into the dining room before a sudden, howling roar, even louder than the hurricane, filled the room. He knew what it was. He'd never been in a tornado before, but he knew what tornadoes sounded like, and he knew that hurricanes spawn tornadoes. There was a tornado somewhere outside, not far off, and it was heading straight toward the house.

He ran back to the room where Carrie was, not caring now if he stumbled over something. Boarded windows were often sufficient protection against a hurricane, but a tornado doesn't even notice the boards are there, any more than it notices brick walls, automobiles, or the tops of shopping centers. A tornado takes out everything in its path.

Carrie, too, had recognized the sound. She had already ripped the sheets and blankets off the bed and wrapped herself in all of it at once to provide as much protection as possible from glass and other flying debris. She lifted one side of the cocoon to allow Quinn in with her, and he grabbed the mattress off the bed and wrapped it as best he could around them.

Danny, upstairs, had also recognized the sound. Like Carrie and Quinn, he had wrapped himself in blankets.

The tornado plowed into the side of the house and kept on coming, bringing with it the mesquite tree, a rowboat it had picked up somewhere else, and what felt like a large amount of the water from West Bay.

"Hold on," Quinn shouted, "we're going for a ride!"

"You ain't took me on the rollie coaster in twenty-five years!" Carrie shouted back.

Inside the laundromat, the body kept moving. Not as fast as it had been, but still moving.

Shigata had felt horror before in his twenty years in law enforcement. He had once been called in to assist a disaster squad in the wake of an airplane crash with two hundred thirty-one dead, seventy-three of them children. He had been tied up and flogged by a terrorist bent on private revenge. He had shot and killed his own first cousin and he had been suspected of murdering his wife by his own adopted daughter.

He could never, in all that time, remember feeling quite the same as he felt watching that rotting corpse inch slowly, in little jerks and starts, over the floor toward him.

If the room had been just a little lighter, it might not have been quite so horrible. If Barlow had turned off his flashlight—the only one on right now—so that it would be just a little darker, he would not have been able to see it . . . but then how much more horrible, to know it was there, to know it must be moving, but not be able to see it and know where it was moving?

He glanced at the others. Joel Moran, too, was watching the corpse. Barlow was looking away from it, but he was game. He hadn't tried to move away from it; he was sitting in the same spot, with his back to it. Southam, sitting between Shigata and Moran with his back toward the rest room door, was looking at it. He had quit talking about Shigata's punching him. He had quit talking about anything. His eyes were glazed with horror.

The body bumped against the corner of the storage room and the head split open. Not the skull, just the skin, which had swollen over the decomposition. Stuff—indescribable stuff—oozed out onto the floor, bringing with it a stench even worse than what was already there.

Jason Southam turned his head, not far enough, and vomited.

"Son of a bitch!" yelled Moran, who suffered the consequences. "You stupid, cowardly son of a bitch!"

But he couldn't have gone out, now now. It was impossible. And this sight, this smell, had even Shigata's mouth dry, his throat burning. Quinn would have vomited if he'd been here, and nobody could call Quinn a coward.

The winds seemed to be easing off. The wall clouds had

passed through headed northeast. Unless by some unimaginable freak of nature the storm reversed a second time, the worst was finally over.

Shigata had to avert their attention from the corpse and from Southam's mishap, or everyone would be sick. He turned on his flashlight, opened the purse, and located the driver's license. "Katy Jester," he read aloud, along with her address.

He searched through the billfold, with Moran now holding the flashlight. There was no name of anyone to notify in case of emergency.

"Damn," he said. He tucked everything neatly back into the billfold and put the billfold back into the purse. He then slowly stood up and stepped out from behind the washers to see whether it was possible yet to get into the wind without being knocked over.

It wasn't.

"Are we still alive?" Carrie asked.

"I think so," Quinn said. "But keep your head down."

They were on the ground in the mud and the rain, still wrapped in the blanket. If they tried to unwrap themselves from the blanket, or tried to stand up, if they even tried to get their heads any higher than was required to keep from drowning, they would be running the risk that the wind would catch them again.

They had put the camera, Shigata's notes and sketches, and the suitcase full of evidence in Shigata's car before he left. So those things were safe, at least as long as Shigata was safe. But all the other evidence was probably scattered over two-thirds of Galveston County.

Quinn said so, and Carrie said, "Never mind the evidence. Think of them three poor girls."

"There's nothing anybody can do for them now. Nothing

but find out who killed them. I'm thinking about any other potential victims of that maniac."

"That's what you do have to think about, isn't it? I never thought of it that way."

"What way?" Quinn, now aware of intense pain in his left wrist, had lost his own train of thought.

"About the other girls he might go after."

The next girls he intended to go after were huddled together under the bridge. Mellissa had heard the tornado; straight across the fields, she was less than a mile from Quinn. Like Quinn and Carrie, she had nowhere to go to get away from a tornado, but she had no pile of bedding to wrap herself in—only the blankets from the car, and the canvas that was supposed to be a tent, which they had used more as a ground cloth to protect themselves from the worst of the rubbish and filth under the bridge.

There was no place to go, no place to hide, and no protection. If the tornado came this way, Melissa and Gail would die. That was all.

In silent terror, Melissa clutched Gail so hard that Gail awoke. She sat up, struggling against Melissa's arms, and cried, "What's that noise?"

"It's the hurricane," Melissa said.

"Why did it get so loud? It wasn't that loud before."

"Sometimes storms get louder and sometimes storms get quieter."

"I want Daddy!" Gail wailed. "I want my daddy—why didn't we stay home? Why did we come up here?"

"This wasn't where we were going," Melissa said helplessly. "We didn't mean to stop here. The car got a flat tire."

"We could have stayed in the car!"

"That wouldn't have done any good. The car floated away, remember?"

"But it floated!" Gail insisted. "It didn't sink. It floated. I saw it. It didn't sink and it didn't fall into the ocean. It stopped at the dike. Last time the rain stopped I could see it. You said it was going to fall into the ocean and it didn't."

"Yet."

"What?"

At least Gail has quit crying. I'd rather she argue than cry.

"It hadn't fallen into the ocean yet, last time we saw it, but it may well be in the ocean now. We couldn't stay in the car, Gail."

"We could have stayed at *home.*"

"Yes, we could have, and if there's another hurricane either we'll leave two days earlier or else we'll stay home. We'll never get caught like this again. Come on, baby. Let's go back to sleep."

If I stay flat on the ground and slither like a snake, I can get to the garage. The cop and the bull dyke can't get there because it's locked, and I have the key.

In this storm, they won't hear the door open and close. They'll only know they're not in the garage. And can't get in.

He'd managed to hold on to the cleaver. Still holding it, he crawled through the mud. His stomach hurt some, but that was all right.

The portable radio was gone. For all Quinn knew, it might have blown into the next county. To get on the air, he'd have to get to the car, and he wasn't sure how he was going to manage to accomplish that.

On second thought, he knew how. The answer was obvious. He was going to crawl. If he could get up on his knees without being blown over. If he couldn't, he was going to wriggle on his belly.

Last time I was wriggling on my belly through the mud somebody was shooting at me, and I got separated from my unit and wound up a POW. I'm in no danger of becoming a POW now, and I don't exactly think anybody's going to shoot at me, but I sure as hell wish I knew where that meat cleaver was.

I wish I could see more than three inches in front of my face. And I wish my wrist didn't hurt so bad.

"Carrie?"

"Yeah?"

"We're going to try to get to the car."

"Okay."

There was no way in hell to drive the Bronco yet, but a low-profile vehicle, like a regular police car, could move now—at very low speeds, and very carefully.

"Moran," Shigata said, "if I leave now, can you take charge of the body? Get it transported and all?"

"Yeah," Moran said. "I don't know when, and I'll be tied up here if you find another one."

"We shouldn't be finding another one," Shigata said, hoping he was not being overly optimistic.

"What I want to know, though, is how you expect to leave."

"Barlow is going to give me his keys, and I'm taking that car. Barlow, don't be in a hurry. I'll let dispatch know you're ten-six. Wait here with Moran until the wind is down enough for you to drive a high-profile car safely. Then take my car to the station and wait for me."

Assuming the station is still standing. I should have thought of that before I sent those kids there. But what else was I going to do? What the hell else was I going to do?

"Southam," Shigata added, "you can leave now if you drive very carefully."

Southam didn't answer. He just got up and headed into

the still-stiff wind for the door. He didn't look again at the corpse.

Shigata held out his hand for Barlow's radio, and Barlow—he was definitely going to be a good cop, once he got over being diffident around authority—handed it over. "Car one to headquarters."

"Headquarters, go ahead."

So the building is still standing. Eve sounds relatively calm, all things considered.

"I'll be ten-eight in about five. I'm going to be en route to the PD in Barlow's car. Barlow is going to be ten-six in my car. Don't give him any calls until he goes ten-eight, because he can't drive that Bronco yet."

"Ten-four," she said, very properly. "Car one, I can't raise Quinn."

"You what?" Shigata said sharply.

"I can't raise Quinn. I've been trying for about five minutes."

"Maybe the batteries on his radio are going out," Shigata said, trying to ignore the uneasy feeling in his stomach.

"It was just fine half an hour ago."

"Have you got any unit in that part of town?"

"No, sir. That's fourteen's beat and she's in here."

"Ten-four. Okay. I'm not going to the station after all. I'll be en route to Quinn's last reported location."

"What's going on?" Moran asked.

Only then did Shigata realize that because of the attempts to keep Southam from knowing of the three dead interns, the medical examiner's office had also been kept from knowing. That was a breach of protocol. It might even be illegal.

"Barlow, I'm changing your assignment a little," Shigata said. "I want you to stay here with this body until we can get somebody out here to pick up. Then remain here until I tell you to secure the scene and leave. Can you do that?"

"Yes, sir."

"Moran, I want you to come with me."

"What for?"

"I'll tell you in the car."

"Chief?" Barlow said. "Can you wait just a minute before you leave?"

"Sure, why?"

"I want to check these doors."

I want to get to Quinn, now. But I'm the chief of the whole department. That was what I told Quinn before I took the job, when he kept reminding me the department needed a chief. We were already friends, but I knew he didn't much like authority, and I said, "Al, if I become chief I'll be chief. You've got to understand that."

He grinned at me and answered, "That's the general idea."

We were talking about authority, then, about my giving orders and his taking them. I wasn't thinking that I might have to leave him to die while I did something else.

Not that. Please not that.

Barlow was walking around, fairly briskly considering he was having to keep his balance in a strong wind, checking doors. All were closed. All except the rest-room door were locked.

He opened the rest-room door. There was nobody inside.

He stepped over the body to reach the office door. He didn't like stepping over the body, but it didn't tear him out of the frame. The body was a body. Nobody lived there anymore. He just wanted to know what was behind those doors.

He looked to Shigata for permission. Shigata nodded, and Barlow put his full weight against the office door. It was a cheap lock, and it popped open at once. There was nobody in the office. There was nobody in the storage room.

Barlow sat down on the floor with his back to the back wall of the building, just where Moran had been sitting earlier. He was much nearer the body than anybody wanted to be, but he was in absolutely the safest place in the entire building. Nobody could slip up on him from behind or from either side, and if they came from the front he would see them before they saw him.

The only way anybody could get to him unseen was to come through the back door, on the north wall right between the rest room in the northeast corner and the three huge extractor washers that filled the north wall to the place where the storeroom started. But nobody could come in that way without making a lot of noise breaking down doors, because that door led into the back of the laundromat owner's house, which faced the opposite street. The owner's house was locked and boarded up, and the owner had obviously had the sense to head northwest out of the hurricane's path. Nobody was coming through there with a key.

Even over the storm Barlow would hear somebody breaking in doors.

"We're going now," Shigata said.

"Right."

In the car, Moran said, "You're bound to have a good reason for taking me away from a body."

"I do."

"You want to tell me what it is?"

"Three more bodies."

Moran cursed.

It was farther from wherever they had landed to the car than Quinn had expected it was going to be. He didn't even know exactly which direction the tornado had come from. He did know that the pain in his left wrist was rapidly becoming unbearable, and he couldn't stop using the wrist because there was no way, yet, that he could get up and walk.

I'm responsible for protecting this crime scene, which has been blown all over the map. I'm responsible for protecting this civilian, who is probably—at least I hope—in better shape than I am. And I'm responsible for protecting myself. I've lost my radio, and I can't even draw my gun much less fire it since I have a broken wrist and I'm heading into shock. I have to get to the car fast.

But when I do get to the car, what do I expect to do then? I think I've lost my car keys. Besides that, I don't know which way the car is.

I can't have lost my car keys. They are on a clip on my belt. How could anything get blown off a clip on my belt?

A friend who was in the Marines told me she put on her dog tags when Camille hit Mississippi. She wanted them to be able to identify her body if it came to that. The dog tags blew off her neck; she found them three days later, driven into a pine tree.

A broom straw was driven in beside them.

A broom straw.

My wrist hurts. My wrist hurts. My wrist hurts.

The pain filled his skull with something that was white and jangled and tasted like copper and bile. He didn't know where Carrie was. He didn't know where the meat cleaver was, or the guy who had taken the meat cleaver.

I'm on the driveway now. I can't stop on the driveway because when somebody comes looking for me—and somebody will—they won't be able to see me on the driveway when they drive up. I don't want Shigata to run over me. I don't want to be killed by my best friend.

He put out his hand to move just a little farther. The car had to be somewhere near here, unless the tornado had picked it up and carried it away, and he didn't think it had because there wasn't more than the normal hurricane debris here, just roof tiles and tree limbs and uprooted fig trees, but fig trees don't have very deep roots anyway, not like mesquites, their roots go clear to China, was it an earlier tornado they hadn't recognized that uprooted the mesquite and thrust it through the window, but he had to get a little farther, maybe under the car—that would be a good place. He caught hold of something to pull on, caught hold with his left hand, and someone or something touched him from behind and the pain rose up to fill his skull completely.

If I can get some rope, I can drop down from the road and get under the bridge before the water goes down. That way I don't have to wait another day.

There was a rope at the other place. He'd just have to go and get it, and to go and get it he'd have to get to his truck.

He might have to put the cleaver down. But he didn't want to put the cleaver down. He looked at it. There was blood on it. It must be pretty fresh blood, not to have washed out in all this rain.

Now how did that get there?
Am I forgetting things again?
My stomach hurts.

Through lightning bolts in the wet darkness, Carrie saw the truck leave, a truck that didn't belong in the garage. The truck she'd last seen the night the girls were killed.

She'd managed to hold on to her pistol through everything. She raised it now and fired.

I'm a tough old battle-ax. I know how to use a pistol. I shouldn't miss.

She didn't miss. She heard the sound of metal striking metal at a terrific speed, but hitting the cab wasn't hitting the driver. She fired again and again. The truck drove on, out of the driveway. The last glimpse of it she had, it was turning toward town.

Damn. Now I've got to find Al. Don't know where the hell he went. Don't know how in hell he went anywhere, on his hands and knees with that broken bone sticking partway out of his wrist.

It ought not to take over twelve minutes to get from the laundromat in downtown Bayport to the garish blue house on Bayshore Drive. It ought not to take over twenty-five minutes to drive from one side of the city to the other across the widest spot, at its widest point, with the twenty-mile-an-hour school zone lights turned on.

In normal circumstances.

When he was in the FBI his jurisdiction was the United States and all its territories; his beat often took in several states. But now it was shrunk to this. One very small town in a fairly small county of what hadn't for a very long time now been the largest state.

It wasn't too small. It wasn't ever too small. But right now it was too large; right now Bayport, Texas, felt bigger than the state of Alaska.

Shigata kept having to detour, to stop, wait, study the road and the things on the side of the road, none of which he could see very well because it was pitch-dark with no moon, stars, or anything else except his own headlights, to see or figure out how deep the water on the road was and whether he could get through it. He'd been driving twenty-five minutes and he wasn't much closer to Quinn than he'd been when he had left the laundromat.

His eyes ached from the strain of peering through the darkness, and they burned with that terrible salt-filled dryness that comes from unshed tears.

Periodically, he heard the dispatcher saying the same thing: "Headquarters to car thirty-one. Car thirty-one, please respond. Headquarters to car thirty-one." Car thirty-one did not respond.

They passed a pickup truck that was heading toward

town. It was so dark the only way they could tell it was a truck was by the shape of its headlights and the fact that they were farther apart and higher than the headlights on a car were. Probably headed for the emergency room, Shigata thought.

He drove on. It was after eleven o'clock now. He hoped somebody had tucked those boys into the empty cots at the police station. It was a sure thing no police were going to be using them.

The wind was down enough now that the truck wouldn't get blown off the road. And he really wanted the rope. They'd bought a whole roll of it. The old man had said Danny could keep the other place, the place Mother had lived. The old man didn't want it anymore—all he wanted was out of it.

They'd bought the rope to tie down the trunk of the car over the things the old man took with him. None of Mother's stuff—Danny had made sure of that—just the stuff the old man brought with him when he moved in.

He would use the rope to get to the women. The blond women. The woman and the girl, who were wanton like all the others. Them. More of Them. He would kill all Their women.

He passed a car. The car was going the other way, back toward the houses and the bridge the women were under. He almost panicked, but then he remembered They couldn't get under the bridge, not until the water was gone. He would be able to, because he had the rope, but They wouldn't have any rope.

The rope was at the house, the house behind the laundromat. Mother's laundromat. His laundromat, now.

*   *   *

If the car hadn't been practically crawling, Shigata would never have been able to recognize the driveway. Almost all the landmarks that were close enough to be visible through the downpour had been blown away. As it was, he couldn't see the house at all. It was as if the night and the wind and the rain had swallowed it.

Oddly enough, the rural mailbox, which would have seemed most likely to have been knocked down by the first gust of wind, was still standing—a little drunken in appearance, but present. So this was definitely the right driveway.

AS HE HEADED UP THE LONG DRIVEWAY, HE felt something bump and crunch under the wheels and wondered what it was. It could be anything, in this storm; debris was everywhere.

He drove on, looking for the police car, looking for the house. He should have been able to see the house by now. He'd have to go in the rear door, he remembered, because the front door was jammed with that mesquite tree.

Through the almost continual lightning, Shigata could see Quinn's police car, sitting in the driveway exactly where it had been parked. He knew exactly where the car was in relation to the house. He took another careful look.

He could see where the house had been. He could see well enough to realize that there was no trick of the lightning, no trick of the clouds or the rain, hiding it.

The house was not there. What was there was a heap— not even a very large heap—of collapsed rubble.

He got out of the car and, oblivious now to the rain, walked toward the debris. Vaguely, he heard Moran get out on the other side of the car.

He stood in the rain, looking through the darkness at where the house had stood. Moran stopped beside him.

"Quinn was in there?"

"Yeah."

Moran had known Quinn longer than Shigata had, though never as well.

"Shit. Where do we start?"

Shigata shook his head.

He stood a moment longer, then said, "We start with hoping." He walked toward the other police car, the one Quinn had been driving.

"Shigata?"

It wasn't Quinn's voice. It was a woman. Carrie. The wind hadn't quite let up enough for him to be able to run yet, but he walked fast toward the sound. She didn't shout again.

Carrie and Quinn were sitting on the ground wrapped in a soaking wet blanket, their backs to the police car. Quinn was slumping rather than sitting, and his eyes were closed.

"What happened?" Shigata asked, kneeling in the mud beside Quinn and touching his head to check the pulse at his temple. It was reassuringly strong and steady.

"Tornado," she said, and pointed to the rough bandage—strips torn off a sheet, it looked like—on Quinn's wrist. "The son of a bitch got away," she added.

"Somebody did this—" Shigata heard shock in his voice and wondered why. He'd certainly been seeing worse than a damaged wrist.

"No, he got this when the house blew down. And then the damn fool tried to crawl on it and 'course he passed out cold. I had to drag him over here. No, but that kid, the one in the truck with the jacked-up tires, he was here. I saw him driving off. Shot at him but missed, with this damn-fool weather."

The truck that passed us going into town.

"Let's get him to my car," Shigata said. "Moran, will you—"

Moran helped. Carrie opened doors. Then Shigata gave Moran Quinn's car keys.

"You might as well drive it in. There's nothing for you to do here. We won't even be able to find the bodies till tomorrow or the next day."

"Okay," Moran said. "I think I'll poke around here a little, though. Might find something. Anyway, I want to wait for the water to go down a little more. Don't wait for me—get him on to the hospital."

There are places you doze off. A deserted laundromat, with no electricity, in the middle of a hurricane, in close proximity to the decaying corpse of a murdered woman, is not one of those places.

All the same, Ted Barlow had worked an eighteen-hour day. Even a healthy young man with a vivid imagination can get very, very tired. So he'd been half-dozing, but he was thoroughly awake now, awake and wondering exactly what he ought to do—because he was absolutely certain there was somebody moving around in the house that backed up to the laundromat.

There was no alley between them, just a wall; you could unlock the door and step right from the house into the laundromat. That was the one door he hadn't gone through, because there was really no reason to. Besides that, all the other locks here were trash, but that door had a deadbolt on it. He hadn't liked not knowing what was on the other side of that door, but if anybody was going to come in chances were that they'd come in the street door, which couldn't be relocked after Shigata's manipulations. If he had to have his face to one door and his back to another he'd rather have his back to that door and his face to the street door.

That was the decision he'd make. He hadn't been happy about it. There was never a cop alive who wanted his back to any door.

It doesn't always—it doesn't often—start out as a conscious fear. It's just, you learn fast that you want to know who is coming in that door. Always. It starts out as a habit. But it doesn't take it long to become a conscious fear.

There's that saying, threatened men live long. But cops learn that isn't always true. Maybe the fiftieth time somebody says, "I'll get you," it doesn't matter as much as the first time. But always, always, always there's that lurking possibility that somebody, sometime, might really try. So you don't sit with your back to the door.

Now, Barlow thought it over and made a careful decision. There was one place from which he could watch both doors and not be vulnerable to somebody entering through either one. Actually there were two, but the other would involve moving the corpse to get where she was. He didn't really think he wanted to try that. At least not by himself.

So that left only one place: the rest room. From the rest room he didn't have a good view of the front door, but he had a perfect view of the door to the house. Anybody entering that way would have to walk right past the rest room to reach any place at all in the laundromat.

It was possible that he was borrowing trouble. Perhaps he wasn't hearing a person at all; perhaps he was hearing no more than a bad roof leak or something like that. Or perhaps he really was hearing a person walking around but that person was only the owner come back early from wherever he or she had gone to, to escape the storm.

That suggestion was whistling in the dark and Barlow knew it. He had lived in this area all his life. He knew of at least one, often two, places on every road out of here that wouldn't be passable for another day or more. And nobody was going to come back by helicopter to check a laundromat.

Even assuming you could land a helicopter here yet, which Barlow very seriously doubted.

He had no doubt now that he was hearing footsteps in the house. They were coming closer.

My stomach hurts.

The rope wasn't in the house. He'd looked all the places in the house the rope ought to have been and it wasn't in any of them.

He knew the old man hadn't taken the rope with him because it was Danny's rope and the old man knew not to take anything that belonged to Danny or to Danny's mother. So the rope had to be around somewhere. If it wasn't in the house, then it had to be in the laundromat. In the storeroom in the laundromat.

That wouldn't be too bad. She was in the front of the laundromat, if they hadn't found her yet, and of course if they had found her then they would have taken her away.

It was her fault, all of it. She was the cause of it, to start with— all the others came later. Of course, the old man said that wasn't true. He said he hadn't met her until later, a long time later, and even then he'd met her by accident.

But I know better than that. I had watched her for years, coming to the laundromat, washing underwear with lace on it and folding it on that table out for everybody to see, tossing her blond hair and talking and smiling to everybody. Not like a decent, modest woman. Nothing decent and modest about her.

No telling how long it had been going on before I found out about it, before Mother died of it.

It was about that time she quit using the laundromat. Quit for a couple of years and then came back. Of course, she and the old man had been meeting on the sly those years. I knew that, even if the old man thought I didn't.

The old man had the nerve to ask me to help fix her washer. I even went over there a time or two, mainly to make sure she was as bad as I'd thought. And she was, no possible doubt of it. Dressing in bright colors, running around in short clothes in front of him.

So she had to be the first to die, and that was right, that was reasonable.

He just hadn't planned on going back in again until after they'd found her and taken her away. It was going to smell pretty funny in there.

My stomach hurts.

He had to get the rope. If he didn't get the rope, the one under the bridge might get away, and something awful would happen if she did. He didn't know what, but something. Something awful.

With the cleaver in his hands again he unlocked the door that led into the laundromat.

Barlow heard the little click as the lock released. He drew his service revolver and held it up and ready so he could lower it into shooting position fast if he needed to. He stood still, breathing deeply, ready to hold his breath for complete silence if he needed to.

Somebody came through the door. It was a man, wearing brown slacks and a yellow shirt, with short brown hair and a pudgy, not unpleasant, face. In his left hand he was carrying a flashlight and in his right hand he was carrying a bloodstained meat cleaver.

That apparition, at midnight in a hurricane, would probably be sufficient to cause most reasonable people to fire their weapon, but Barlow was observant. Not only did he observe things, he observed them quickly.

The man's clothes were soaked and covered with mud, but there was also blood on his shirt and pants, and more blood was dripping out with each heartbeat. If he had wanted to, Barlow could have counted his pulse by the spurts of blood.

His abdomen had been laid open as neatly as if he were in the middle of surgery. The wound was neither long nor deep, but it was long enough and deep enough that one coil of intestine was peeking through, along with some kind of tissue and something else that bulged and pulsed and was sort of purple and blue. The wound was exactly the length of the blade of the meat cleaver. He'd laid his own belly open.

Barlow didn't know how the man managed to stay on his feet.

Why in the world would anybody, no matter how crazy he was, want to do that, or was it an accident? Maybe he was so deep in shock he didn't even realize yet that he had done it.

Barlow considered all this so quickly that before he was done thinking he had stepped neatly out of the rest room and taken the meat cleaver out of the man's hand. The man screamed, the loudest scream Barlow had ever heard in his life.

"It's all right," Barlow yelled. "I'm here to help you. It's all right. I'll call you an ambulance."

The man went on screaming. The only words Barlow could make out were "No—no—no—no—" The more he screamed the more the blood bubbled out of his intestines.

Barlow had the cleaver and his own gun. There was nothing the man could do now but run, and he wouldn't get very far if he did. Barlow had to call for help, but there was no way on earth he could make himself heard through that steady screaming. He had to get a little ways away from it.

Radio in hand, he walked toward the front of the store to radio for help.

Shigata heard a confused moan in the back seat, followed by the small rustling sounds of someone moving around, and then the muttered word "Damn!" Not much, but enough to tell him Quinn was conscious and had figured out where he was.

"How are you feeling?"

"Like shit." Quinn's voice was slurred. "I didn't feel it to start with, but after I did start feeling it I sure should have had better sense than to try to crawl with it. Did Carrie tell you about the meat cleaver?"

"Uh-uh. Did you land on one? Is that what happened to your wrist?"

"No. He's got one."

"Who's got one?"

Carrie told Shigata about the meat cleaver.

"You better tell me again about the man who rented the upstairs apartment," Shigata said. "How long has he had it? How old is he? What does he look like? Ben Cummings, didn't you say that was his name?"

"Ben Cummings, yeah," Carrie said. "Look, he didn't do this."

"People nobody thinks could have done it have done stranger things than this a lot of times before now," Quinn said, his voice a little stronger. "Somebody was upstairs in that apartment tonight."

"You tried to convince me there wasn't."

"I didn't want to scare you."

"What are you, some kinda jackass?" Carrie demanded. "I had a .357 Magnum."

"I heard you when you were shooting through the door,

and I saw you when you opened the door. Don't try and tell me you weren't scared."

"Okay, so I was scared, so what? If you heard somebody up there you should have gone and checked."

"I was trying to," Quinn pointed out reasonably. "It wasn't my fault I couldn't get there. 'Course, if that was Ben Cummings he might be dead."

"I'm telling you, it wasn't Ben Cummings up there, and whoever was there isn't dead. He drove off in that pickup truck with the jacked-up tires. Drove right over you, with you laying passed out on the driveway. You were laying just right so he missed you with all four wheels. Drove out the driveway and turned right and headed toward town."

"How long before I drove up was that?" Shigata asked quickly.

She told him.

"That was the truck I passed."

He could hear Quinn, in the back seat, trying to sit up. "You mean he's headed into town?"

"It would appear that way."

"Then we'd better warn—"

"Wait a minute," Carrie said. "Warn who about who? I'm telling you, that was *not* Ben Cummings in that truck. Ben Cummings hasn't even got a truck."

"Okay," Shigata said. "Okay. Tell me about Ben Cummings."

"He works for an insurance company. Not a salesman, some kind of—I don't know what you call it. He drives around and looks at things to see if whatever was supposed to have happened really did. He's, oh, about forty-seven, something like that. His wife died about five years ago. He got engaged to another woman a few months ago and his stepson carried on like a crazy thing and he finally decided he'd better move out. That's why he rented the place from me. Found out about it from Dan Weston. Weston had been his wife's doctor and they'd kind of gotten to be friends. He told me he wanted a furnished place because he wasn't going to stay long, said he would move in with his girlfriend as soon as they got married. The stepson kinda settled down as soon as he moved out, started acting a little friendlier again, but Ben said he didn't want to move back in with him. He figured he'd be better off with me."

The wheels were turning in Mark Shigata's head. "What's the girlfriend's name? Did he ever tell you?"

"Oh, now, what was it? Rita? No, that's not right. I just met her once. Katy, that was it. Katy. I can't think of her last name."

"Think you might recognize it?" Shigata asked.

"Oh, yeah, I might."

He picked a couple of names at random. "Williams? Rogers?"

She said no to each of those.

"Jester?"

"Jester! That was it, Katy Jester. Real pretty girl. She had this long blond hair, you know, not phony blond but real blond, and she kept it straight, the way girls used to wear it when we was kids."

"Do you remember Ben's stepson's name?"

"Sure," she said promptly. "Danny. His name was Danny."

"Danny what?"

"Now that's silly. I was thinking Danny Cummings but 'course it wasn't Cummings because Ben's his stepfather, not his father. You know, I don't think I ever did hear his last name. Danny. That's all I know."

It was impossible, completely impossible. A man with his abdomen laid open with a meat cleaver does *not* walk off while the closest cop is calling for an ambulance. Or if he does, he at least doesn't walk far.

The man wasn't in the laundromat by the time Barlow got off the radio. More afraid than he had been in a long time, Barlow went through the door into the house. He searched it from top to bottom, including inside closets and under beds, with an ambulance driver helping him. The man wasn't there. He'd left the front door of the house open, and where he'd gone from there, somebody might know, but Barlow sure as hell didn't.

The ambulance people decided that since they were here, they might as well take the body, since it had already been photographed and measurements wouldn't do a bit of good now. So they took the body away, which meant that Barlow was no longer sitting in the dark with a decaying corpse. But they didn't take the smell away.

Barlow had the man's meat cleaver, but there was no telling what other weapons he might come back with. He'd seen the man's eyes. That man was insane. Ted Barlow had no doubt about that.

So it was not, he considered, unreasonable for him to be afraid on a night like this, even armed as he was.

He wanted to go out and get in the chief's Bronco and lock the doors, but he didn't. He sat in the laundromat, huddled in the corner between the office door and the storeroom door, where there was no possible way for anybody to approach him from any direction except dead front. He waited for the dawn, for somebody to come and relieve him and tell him he could go somewhere that didn't stink and didn't have maniacs running around with meat cleavers. Someplace where he could get something to drink and then get some sleep.

He didn't want anything to eat right now.

*　　*　　*

Quinn cried out once, from the pain, when Shigata went to help him out of the back seat of the car, but he jeered at the suggestion that somebody could get him a wheelchair or stretcher—"It ain't my leg that's broke, it's my wrist"—and insisted on walking in under his own steam.

I'm the chief of police. This isn't a private situation. I would like to stay with Quinn while the doctors check him. But I have a job to do, and he knows that as well as I do.

Shigata went to the rest room and washed off the worst of the mud. There wasn't much he could do about the fact that he was completely drenched. Feeling cleaner, if not otherwise less rumpled, he went to find out what room Weston had been put in. He went up the stairs, because the sign on the elevator said, "Do not use during emergency power situations unless necessary."

As he went up the stairs, he thought about a lot of things. First, about how thankful he was Melissa had finally decided to leave, even if it was later than he wanted her to. If he had to worry about her and Gail now, with all of this going on . . . well. One man can do only so much and he was pushing closer to the breaking point than he liked to think about.

It was about one-thirty in the morning now and he'd have to stop and think to determine how long it had been since he had slept. He didn't have time to figure it out now. The fact that he didn't probably made it unnecessary to try.

At least they were safe.

Second, about the case. There are things you do when you are working a case, especially a complicated one. You check your own records. You talk to neighbors. There are a lot of things you do.

In this storm, he couldn't do any of them.

Richard Weston was asleep in hospital pajamas, in a properly made up bed.

Damn! I wonder where his clothes are? I should have collected them. That bloodstain on his knee, that splash on his shoulder, they don't mean what I thought they meant at first, but they damn sure mean something.

Dan Weston was asleep on the other bed in the room, fully clothed except for his shirt and shoes. Dave Lueders was dozing in a chair by the door.

Shigata did what any cop would do under the circumstances. He woke Lueders first and let Lueders wake Weston. Dan, not Richard. Considering what he knew of Richard's condition, waking him might not be such a very good idea.

"I wanted to ask you about the victims," Dan said. "Because if they're who I think they might be then I might have an idea about the motive."

"Who do you think they are?" Shigata asked.

"Judy Grey and Josie Martinez."

"Why did you think it might be them?"

"They live with Gwen. I was thinking about a motive. What would make somebody want to kill Jean and go after Gwen? I have an idea."

"What's your idea?"

"Was it Judy and Josie?"

"Yes. We think the third was Terra Camacho, but we aren't certain on that one yet."

Dan Weston shut his eyes. "Damn. Damn it all to hell and gone."

"I don't know Terra Camacho," Richard Weston said, sitting up, a little shaky.

"Shut up," Dan Weston said. "You're not supposed to be talking."

"I still don't know Terra Camacho. Don't be an ass, Dan. I'm not supposed to be getting excited, not I'm not supposed to be talking." Richard's face was pale and his speech slightly slurred, either from his condition or plain fatigue.

"I'm afraid I'm a little too human to lie here in bed and hear that one half of my research team has been wiped out, say ho-hum, and go back to sleep. They didn't deserve that— they were nice girls. But Terra Camacho wasn't—"

"On the research team," Dan finished. "Yes, I know Terra Camacho. Very vaguely. She's an intern in pediatrics. Main reason I know her is because she's damn near a ringer for Gwen, so I noticed her and asked who she was. I thought she might be kin to Gwen but she and Gwen both said she wasn't."

"What was she doing in Gwen's apartment?" Shigata asked.

Dan shrugged. "Maybe getting off the Island. Gwen had left for East Texas to spend a week with a sick relative. She wasn't supposed to be back yet. I guess she got all responsible and decided to come back early because of the storm, figuring she'd be needed. She's that kind of person."

"But Terra—"

"I'm getting to that," Dan said. "If Terra didn't want to run the risk of staying on the Island but did want to stay in the area, then she knew where there was a vacant bed. That's what she would have been doing at Gwen's apartment. My guess is she was murdered because she was there. And because she looked like Gwen, but mainly just because she was there. You can't kill two girls in an apartment and walk off and leave the third, now can you?"

"So what do you think was the motive?"

"The research team."

"The research team," Shigata repeated.

"Yeah. We were doing research on AIDS. Richard was telling you something about that already, I think. The AIDS virus does a lot of damage to the brain. Well, we're neurosurgeons, but a neurosurgeon is also a neurologist. Do you know what a neurologist does?"

"I think so."

"A lot of people think of neurosurgeons as brain surgeons. We are, but that's not all. We study diseases of and injuries to the entire nervous system, not just the brain, although the brain is of major significance. We also work with the spinal cord and all the various connections. I'm trying to put this into layman's terms and I hope it makes sense."

"It does," Shigata said.

"Well, it's reasonable to assume that something that's doing damage to the brain is doing damage to the entire central nervous system. We wanted to try to determine *exactly* what the virus was doing and how it was doing it, in hopes that we could figure out some way to combat it. Richard and I were running the project. We had another neurologist on it, and three interns working as research assistants. Gwen, Judy, and Josie."

"Six people," Shigata said.

"Six people. Okay, so it wasn't half the team knocked out, it was a third of the team. That still doesn't exactly light up my galaxy."

"All right, you had a research project designed to determine how the AIDS virus harms the brain and the central nervous system and what could be done about it," Shigata summarized. "Who's going to object to that? Agreed, we all know about gay-bashing, but killing members of a research team, and the wife of one member, would be a little farfetched, even for the most determined gay-basher."

"That doesn't have anything to do with it," Weston said. He wiped his forehead and said, "Excuse me," got up from the bed, went to the rest room, and shut the door.

Shigata heard water running. Weston returned a moment later with a slightly damp face.

"I'm sorry. This is a little hard to handle. I'm doing the best I can. You know what an *in vitro* experiment is?"

"Is that where you try to keep body tissue living while you do experiments on it?"

"Yeah," Weston said. "Now, we were trying to keep some brain cells alive *in vitro* to work with. Remember, these are brain *cells,* not an entire brain, and they're absolutely riddled with the AIDS virus. There is no possibility, absolutely no possibility whatever, of any type of consciousness existing."

"Okay."

"And we weren't keeping the samples without permission from next of kin, except in a few cases where some people who were dying who knew about the experiments told us *they* would like to give consent. That's really something, you know, somebody who cares that much about knowledge—"

"Is that a motive for murder?" Shigata interrupted.

"Not usually. But there was this one woman, Margaret Cummings. The one we told you about, that had cancer and got a blood transfusion. Her husband gave consent and her son threw a fit like I never saw before. We could *not* convince him that his mother wasn't still somehow alive in those brain cells. Then he found out about me and Gwen, and he got it into his head that we had, for some reason I never could figure out, murdered his mother. He was accusing Richard and me both of murder, and his father . . . his stepfather . . . of adultery and murder. He got in once and tried to wreck the lab, and we wound up having to bar him from the hospital with a court order. It was a pretty distressing situation."

"What was his name?"

Dan grimaced. "That's another reason I thought of him. Gwen mentioned Danny. She never calls me Danny, just Dan, and whether you knew it or not, *I* knew I hadn't done those things she was talking about. *His* name is Danny."

"Danny what?"

"Damned if I know. It's probably in records."

"Which are presently inaccessible."

"Which are presently inaccessible," Dan Weston agreed. "But I thought you ought to know."

monday, august 28
3:00 a.m.

DANNY WAS BACK IN DAN WESTON'S condo. He didn't remember how he got there.

I unlocked the door to the laundromat and the dead woman rose up and touched me and took the weapon out of my hand. I smelled her and I smelled her death, I smelled the death and decay.

That's what they did to my mother. Killed her, put her in the ground.

I smelled the death and decay and the stench of the grave, and the dead woman rose up and touched me.

I'm hot.

My stomach hurts.

I'm hot and thirsty, and when I try to drink, the water runs out of my shirt and does me no good and I shake when I walk.

The dead woman rose up and touched me, and now I am dead, too. The odor of death and rot is on me. I'm dying inside out. I am dead but still I walk. There is something red and green oozing out of my stomach where the water falls out when I drink. I am dead. But I will take them to the grave with me, all of them I can. That woman under the bridge will be dead with me, and that girl. They will go to wait on my mother.

All of them except three I will kill. I will not kill the two doctors.

I will not kill the old man. All of them will live as I have lived—bereft, alone, knowing those they loved are in the grave and rotting as my mother rotted, as I rot now.

My stomach hurts.

Shigata walked through the emergency room, opening doors and apologizing until he finally opened the right door. Al Quinn, at least temporarily alone, was lying on his back looking at a featureless white ceiling. His wrist, now unbandaged, was bent at an odd angle, and bone was protruding a good three inches. It was hard to see more than that because the open wound was soaking.

When Shigata entered, Quinn turned his head and said, "Hi." Weariness and pain were visible on his face.

"Hi," Shigata said, trying not to stare. He'd known almost as long as he'd known Quinn that Quinn had spent several years as a POW, held by the Vietcong in various, all unpleasant, jungle compounds. This was the first time he'd seen Quinn shirtless.

"You knew it was there," Quinn said, following his thoughts with the ease of long association.

"Yeah. How's the wrist?"

"It's there."

"They give you anything for pain?"

"I'm okay."

"That wasn't what I asked."

"No, they didn't give me anything for pain. Not yet. It doesn't hurt as much as it probably looks like. Anyway, they're fixing to knock me out, soon's they get through figuring out my blood type. I told 'em it's B positive, but they have to test it, anyway. I guess they figure I might not know for sure. But they did take the X rays already. You want the good news first or the bad news?"

"Whatever."

Quinn closed his eyes briefly, then opened them and tried to grin. "Trouble is I don't know which is which."

Shigata waited.

"They can't put me in a cast."

"Of course not, with an open wound."

"Who's telling this, me or you?"

"Go ahead." Shigata found a tall stool, wheeled it over beside Quinn, and sat down on it.

"So they're gonna put a pin in it. I asked what that meant and they showed me this steel rod, looks about six inches long. They said I'll heal pretty quick, a lot quicker than if I did have a cast, but I'll be limited a few weeks. No drivee, no shootee, no fuckee. At least not left-handed."

"You want me to go get Nguyen?"

"Hell no!" Quinn said, in real alarm. "At this time of night? What do you want to do, scare her to death?"

"What time was she expecting you home?"

"She wasn't. I told her I'd be sleeping at the police station. She can't get any TV news, not that this'd be on the TV or the radio, anyway, and if she does get any radio news she'll hear about the murders and figure I'm busy. She doesn't understand English well enough to try to listen to a scanner. So there's no chance she'll find out till tomorrow, and the doctor said barring complications I can go home tomorrow morning, if I promise to go to bed and stay there."

"I'll come by in the morning and get you, then, but I'll bet they tell you to stay here another day."

"If they do, they do." Quinn closed his eyes again. Then he said, abruptly, "This is gonna limit my wrist motion some."

"Yeah, and you'll set off the metal detectors in airports so they'll have to hand-scan you."

"That's not what I'm talking about."

"Then what are you talking about?"

"There is no police department I know of that would hire a man with a limited range of wrist motion."

"Were you planning on going job hunting?"

"Are you misunderstanding me on purpose?"

"I wasn't to start with. I am now. What do you think I am, Al? You think I'm gonna fire my best friend for getting hurt on the job?"

"You won't," Quinn said, "but the city doctor—"

"Won't. Period. Forget it. Not unless the city wants everybody on the department from me on down to the last recruit I hired to walk out. Don't worry. It won't happen."

"Okay," Quinn said. "Now tell me what's going on."

Shigata was still talking when a nurse came in and said, "Sir, you've got to leave now, we have to get him on up to surgery."

"Okay," Shigata said, and stood up. *"Shim-pai-nai,"* he said to Quinn, and Quinn's grin this time was broad and real.

"What does that mean?" the nurse asked.

"It's Japanese for 'good luck' or 'don't sweat it' or something like that," Shigata said.

"Oh." The nurse looked doubtfully at Quinn. "Does he speak Japanese?"

"He does," Shigata answered. *"I'm* the one that doesn't." He stepped out of the way as they moved the bed out rather than try to move Quinn to another bed. "I'm going to see if I can find Gwen and see if she's awake," he added. "I'll see you tomorrow."

The last he saw of Quinn was a right-handed thumbs-up gesture, as the bed departed feetfirst.

There was a good chance, of course, that Gwen Hardesty would not be awake. It was, after all, the middle of the night, and when he'd seen her quite a few hours ago she'd looked down for the count. But if she'd gotten the stuff she'd been fed out of her system, she might well be wide-awake.

As it happened, she was. She was in a room by herself, so if he shut the door they wouldn't be disturbed.

She looked at him in quick alarm as he came in. "Do I know you?"

"No," he said. "I was downstairs when you came in, but you didn't seem to be in much of a state to be noticing anything. I'm Mark Shigata, Bayport chief of police. I know it's the middle of the night, but if you could answer a few questions—"

"About—him?"

Shigata nodded. "About him—and about your roommates. Mind if I sit down?"

"Please do." She got a tissue from a package by the bed, blew her nose. "I don't usually panic. I've actually finished my internship and I'm starting a residency in neurosurgery. I'm usually quite calm and reasonable. But I don't usually walk in on something like that." She wiped her eyes and blew her nose again. "I guess you don't even know what I'm talking about. Or maybe you do. You mentioned my roommates."

"Dan Weston gave us your key. Legally, we couldn't go over there without some sort of paperwork, but due to the situation, we decided the courts would uphold us if we did, anyway."

"I'll sign something retroactively if you want."

"I don't think that would do any good. But if the question comes up—"

"Yes. If the question comes up. They were dead, weren't they?"

"You know they were dead."

"Did you see them?"

"Yes. I don't blame you for reacting as you did."

"Do you know—I don't guess you do."

"I might. What's the question?"

"Who the one in the bathtub is? The one that looks like me?"

"Not for sure. We think she might be Terra Camacho."

"Oh, yeah. That makes sense. Terra does look like me. And she said she might come over while I was gone." Gwen swallowed and blew her nose again. "I guess you think it's pretty stupid of me to carry on like this."

"They were good friends of yours, weren't they?"

"Just about my best friends in the world. We'd gone all through medical school together."

"Well, I'll tell you something, Gwen—may I call you Gwen?" She nodded. "My best friend is on his way into surgery with a broken wrist, and I'm upset enough. If I had to see him the way you saw your friends—well, I don't even want to think about how I'd react. No, the only stupid thing you did was get in there far enough to see Terra and Josie. You should have got out of there as fast as you could as soon as you saw Judy on the couch. Didn't it cross your mind that whoever did it might still be there?"

"Yes, it did. But I had to know. Can't you understand that?"

"Yes. I'm not blaming you."

"Did you see the cocktail glass under Judy's arm?" Gwen asked.

"Yes."

"He—drank from it. He told me."

"Who told you?"

"Danny. I'm sorry. I don't know his last name. Mrs. Cummings's son. Did you talk to Dan—Dr. Dan Weston?"

"Yes. Several times."

"Did he tell you about Danny? I don't guess he did. There'd have been no reason for him to—"

"He did, finally. Tonight. A few other things have happened to make us think of Danny. What more can you tell me?"

"I don't know. I don't know how much you do know, so how can I tell you—"

"Dan Weston told me about the research project, about the brain tissue being kept *in vitro,* about Danny's reaction."

"Did he tell you Danny said we were all murderers, that we'd murdered his mother and now we were torturing her?"

"Part of it. He didn't get into personalities, much. What can you tell me—"

"Personalities." She looked at him. "Whose personalities?"

"Danny's. His mother's. His stepfather's."

"Danny is insane," she said definitely. "I knew that a long time before this happened. I knew it not long after I met him. I mean, people make jokes about men who want to keep women barefoot and pregnant, but he wasn't a joke. He didn't want to keep women barefoot and pregnant, because skin is indecent and so is pregnancy. I don't know what he wanted. An all-male world, maybe."

"Is he gay?"

"No." She shuddered visibly. "He's very, very, very sexually attracted to women, and he thinks that's indecent, and he thinks that women are evil because they make men feel that way. He told me that. About ten thousand times, it felt like, though I guess it wasn't really more than five or six. He told me his stepfather—he kept calling him 'the old man' though I don't know why, because he isn't really very old—was evil, and he accused me of adultery with Dan."

She laughed, the laughter verging on but not quite being hysterical. "I told him if he had to be technical the term was 'fornication,' because I'm not married and neither is Dan, but that made him furious. I was trying to be funny. I didn't try to be funny with him again. He said the old man was committing adultery and that was why we had murdered his mother. That was crazy. Nobody murdered his mother. She died of AIDS. And Cummings struck me as pretty old-fashioned, actually. I'm surprised he's remarrying. Actually, I think that's what he's maddest about, Danny I mean, that and the fact she's blond. He hates blond women. He hates all women but he especially hates women with blond hair. I don't know why, except that his stepfather's new fiancée is blond, but it goes back farther than that, because he hated blond women while his mother was in the hospital and that was way before his stepfather ever *met* his new fiancée. Danny—I hate to call him that because it sounds like a name you would call somebody you like, but I don't know his last name, and I can't call him Dan."

"That's okay," Shigata said. "Call him whatever you need to."

"Well, he just kept saying he was going to kill me, but he was going to kill all the others first. He acted like he thought he was going to kill every blond woman in the world."

Thank God Melissa and Gail are out of his reach. Thank God they left when they did.

"And you don't know why he hates blonds so much."

"No."

"And he kept you prisoner—"

A nurse came in. "Are you aware that it is the middle of the night?" he inquired.

"The thought had crossed my mind," Shigata said.

"Then can't you continue this discussion in the morning?"

Shigata thought about saying no, but the fact was he was very nearly too tired to see straight—and from what he'd heard about the commotion at the laundromat, chances were that Danny wasn't going anywhere else tonight.

"One more question and I'll go," he said.

The nurse looked disapproving but said nothing.

"Do you know anything about a laundromat that had something to do with Danny?"

"Well, yes," she said. "I figured you knew that. It's only a couple of blocks from the police station."

Shigata waited.

"That laundromat on the corner, kitty-cornered from that gun shop that closed down last year," Gwen said. "His mother—Mrs. Cummings—owned it, and the house that backed up to it. When she died, he inherited it. I quit using it. He—the way he *looked* at all the women—" She stopped.

"Thank you," Shigata said. "I may be back tomorrow."

"I hope I'm out of here tomorrow."

Shigata didn't tell her that her apartment was gone. Obviously she had to know, but she'd had enough for one day. He nodded, thanked her again, and went out in the hall. The nurse followed him, turning out the light and closing the door firmly. "May I safely assume we will not see you back here until morning?" he asked.

"You can't safely assume anything," Shigata said. "But I hope I won't be back until morning."

I've got to get some sleep. I'm in charge of this investigation, and with Quinn down I have absolutely no even half-trained investigator to help me. I'm it. But like it or not, I've got to get some sleep.

Shigata drove to the police station through streets a little less flooded than they had been an hour ago. Finding out from the dispatcher who'd been in bed the longest, he routed that person out and sent him to the laundromat to relieve Barlow. He noticed that Barndt was asleep on a cot between two small boys, also on cots. He lay down and turned the lights out in his brain.

Is it worse to have no sleep at all, or too little? Shigata wasn't sure, but he was sure that getting up at six AM after less than three hours of sleep left him with the feeling that his head was stuffed with cotton.

But if he left early enough he could eat breakfast at the hospital; if he waited very long he was not going to be able to eat breakfast at all. Since he hadn't eaten in about twelve hours, he figured he could stand a real breakfast. Then he'd go to see Quinn and offer to take him home, an offer which would not be accepted because the doctors were certainly going to keep him in the hospital at least another day. He would come back to the police station, retrieve the two little boys, and take them to Nguyen until somebody figured out what to do with them.

The sun was back, really, truly back, and the storm was really over. Or rather, the storm had gone north, to dump water on the parched farmland of East Texas. The roads were beginning to dry. By tomorrow, people would be coming back from wherever they'd taken refuge. He'd be able to get out and ask questions. He'd be able to find out more about Danny. He'd clear this case fast, now.

That was the way it was planned. That wasn't quite the way it worked out. Quinn, having had breakfast and somehow managed to scrounge a T-shirt and get his uniform pants back on, was ready to leave.

"The doctors aren't going to make you stay another day?" Shigata demanded.

"Doctors can't *make* me do anything," Quinn said blandly. "There's really no reason for me to stay. I'm not shocky, and they've filled me so full of antibiotics a self-respecting germ would walk a mile to avoid me.''

Shigata laughed. "Okay. You feel like going to the police station to pick up those kids?''

"As long as you're driving.''

Claire Barndt didn't dislike baby-sitting quite as much as she would have liked Barlow to think, but all the same she was glad when Steve and Joey were gone, so she could get back to her regular beat. There had been murders—four of them at least—on her regular beat. Well, she was a patrol officer, she didn't have anything to do with murders. But there was always the possibility she might see that strange man again.

The one she felt was at least possibly the murderer.

Barlow wanted to talk with her over coffee before she went back out on the road. She didn't have time. She really wanted to get back on her beat.

Nguyen was squatting beside a small charcoal burner at the back of the garage, cooking some sort of stir fry and serving it for about eighteen assorted teenagers and children. She stood up and turned when the car drove up. Her face, when Quinn got out with his arm in a sling, was unreadable to Shigata.

Apparently, it was not unreadable to Quinn, because he said, in a rather apologetic tone, "Accident.''

"What kind of accident?'' she demanded.

"I fell out a window.''

"You fell out a window.''

They were looking at each other, that way they had of looking at each other that seemed to exclude the rest of the world. Then, quite unexpectedly to Shigata, they both began to laugh.

"Nguyen, I didn't do it on purpose,'' Quinn chuckled,

his right arm around her waist, which, for once, did not show visible signs of pregnancy.

She said something in Vietnamese, and he laughed again. Then he said, "I see you got the fire outside."

"You tell me to."

"You don't always do what I tell you to."

"I don't wanna suffocate the baby. You tell me charcoal fire inside might suffocate the baby. Who these babies?" she demanded, looking at Steve and Joey. "They wanna come eat?"

"Steve and Joey, this is Mrs. Quinn," Shigata said.

Nguyen crouched so that the boys could see her face more easily. "You call me Nguyen," she said to them. "You gonna come visit me, yeah?"

"For a while," Quinn said. "Their mother is—indisposed." He said something else in Vietnamese.

She looked startled, then said, "Good! I not got enough kids here today. Always need more kids visit me. You come help me? Steve? You name Steve?"

Steve nodded.

"Good! I got boy name Steve, but he seventeen. Got too big to sit on lap. Now, you little enough—no?" Steve was shaking his head. "I bet Joey little enough! You come visit me—Al, you better go lie down. Falling out windows not good."

In the blaze of sunlight, with all the crud from the Texas City refineries washed out of the air by the storm, Claire Barndt could see something wedged in the dike at the curve of Bayshore Road. The roads and the fields were standing in deep water, so she couldn't get close enough to examine it close up, but she did have binoculars in the car. She got them out and studied it.

Then she got on the radio and asked for a records check on a license-plate number.

Shigata heard the request.

"The hell I'm not going with you!" Quinn panted, slamming the car door.

"Get out of the car!" Shigata yelled. "You're in no shape—"

"So I'm a little weak! I'm not gonna fall over. Damn it, Shigata, I'm right-handed! And they've got me so full of antibiotics—"

"You already said that. You're hurting so bad you can't stand up. Don't you think I can tell by looking at you?"

"I know you can tell by looking at me," Quinn said deliberately, "because I've seen you working when you were hurting a hell of a lot worse than I am right now, and you didn't have any antibiotics, and you hadn't had any medical care at all."

"That was different," Shigata muttered.

"Yeah, it was different. Every case is always different. Worst-case scenario—they're gone. I'm going to be with you. Somebody's got to. Best-case scenario—they got out of the car before it got into the water, and that's what I think happened. Then they're out there somewhere on foot and they've got to be found. I can walk."

"You're a damn fool," Shigata said, and started the car. Nguyen stood in the driveway and stared after them, her own baby in one arm and Joey under the other.

The storm was really gone. Melissa and Gail had slept very little over the last two days. Their restless sleep, such as it was, was constantly disturbed by the storm. Now they were both deeply asleep in the shade of the highway bridge. So deeply asleep that the siren of a police car half a mile away did not awaken them.

"That's the way I found it, chief," Barndt said. "There's nobody in it."

"Nobody you can see," Shigata answered, staring through the binoculars.

"The doors are shut, and the windows are rolled up," Barndt said. "There's a flat tire, and the hubcap is off. I think they had a flat, stopped to change it, and for some reason left the car."

Shigata did not answer. He stood and continued to gaze through the binoculars at the car Melissa and Gail had left in.

"Shigata, they're around here somewhere," Quinn said, on the other side of him.

"Maybe," Shigata said. "But in what condition? The son of a bitch hates blonds."

"What?"

"The son of a bitch hates blonds," Shigata repeated. "Melissa was down here. Melissa is a blond. The son of a bitch—Danny whatever his name is—hates blonds."

Quinn took a deep breath and let it out raggedly. "What are you gonna do?"

Shigata shook his head. "I'm chief of the whole department. I can't call everybody off patrol to look for Melissa. Especially not now, when people will be heading back into town and the possibility of looting goes up."

"Some people aren't on patrol."

"What?"

"My sons. My nephews. They'd be glad to help."

Shigata looked back toward the Bronco as if expecting to find it already full of Asian and Eurasian teenagers. But of course it wasn't, and there was nobody he could send.

The Bronco could get through, but a sedan couldn't. Not yet.

The Bronco had to make the trip.

Quinn couldn't drive it, not with his wrist. Shigata could send Barndt, but Quinn's family didn't know her. Most of them would come anyway, because they would accept a message transmitted through her, but probably more would come if he went.

"Let's go," he said.

Conscience smote Claire Barndt. She stepped forward quickly. "Chief. I might have seen the killer."

"What?"

"I tried to tell you yesterday, at the laundromat. I should've made it clearer what I was talking about. But you—too much was going on and you didn't want to listen and I figured it could wait. I shouldn't have. It wasn't over a mile from here."

"Tell me about it."

She told him.

"I should have listened. That was my fault, not yours." He turned and strode toward the Bronco.

"Where are you going?" Quinn demanded.

"To your place. You coming or not?"

Danny, too, had had a very restless night. But he was awake now, looking through the closets in Dan Weston's condo. There must be something there that would help him get to the woman and girl under the bridge.

D ANNY HAD OPENED EVERY DOOR IN THE condo except one, a hall closet that was locked.

If it was locked, there must be something special in it. That made sense. Danny found the hammer he'd used to rip the boards off the window. He began to hammer on the door around the doorknob, around the lock, until he could reach in and open it from the inside.

It was locked from the inside, too. That didn't make sense.

He stopped long enough to drink some water. It had quit falling out now. He supposed that meant something but he wasn't sure what. He wasn't sure of much of anything. He didn't want anything to eat. He was hot and cold at the same time, and there was a bitter-smelling greenish slime dripping from the torn place in his pants. He was shaking all the time, and it was getting harder and harder to get up and walk.

Well, that was to be expected, if he was dead. And he was dead, he knew that. Ever since the dead woman touched him. Even if he didn't know that, he could tell from the smell. The smell was with him all the time now, the smell of the place where people lie dead.

Soon he'd have to lie down, too. Dead people lie down. But he'd get to the one under the bridge first. That was probably going to be the last one. But he'd certainly get her.

He went on hammering around the hinges. He still couldn't get the door open, but he had managed to hammer out a panel of the door, so that he could look in and see what was there.

A lot of things. A backpack. A funny-looking ax. A coil of rope.

So that was it! Dan Weston had been going to get the woman under the bridge. That was why this door was locked, so Danny wouldn't know.

Hands shaking, he disentangled the coil of rope from the frame of the backpack.

"I thought we were going to my place," Quinn said. "I ain't going back into the hospital."

"Then sit in the car," Shigata retorted. "We *are* going by your place, but first I'm going up to talk with Gwen again."

"In that case I'll come with you. I've never seen Gwen."

Last night's nurse had been replaced by a petite blond who looked somewhat startled to see two armed men—one of them in dirty plainclothes, the other in very dirty uniform pants, an old T-shirt, a bandage, and a two-day growth of beard—dashing onto her floor. Shigata flashed his badge. She nodded, but still objected when Shigata, finding Gwen asleep, went to wake her up.

"Now wait a minute—"

Shigata ignored her. "Gwen, wake up—I'm sorry to wake you, but I need some information."

She opened her eyes, looked at him, and sat up. "What time is it?" Her voice was slurred.

"Almost eight-thirty," Shigata said. "You need some water? Sergeant Quinn and I need some information—fast."

"Get me some water."

Working hard at appearing far more calm than he felt, Shigata poured a glass of water and handed it to her.

"Thanks," she said. "Could you—uh—leave the room a minute? I've sort of got to go, and these hospital gowns—"

"Come on," Shigata said to Quinn.

They waited outside until she called them back in. "What do you need to know?" she asked.

"A car has just been found in the Bayshore Road area. It got caught in the flood and washed down to the dike; it's jammed in the dike now, but it appears to have been abandoned before the flood. It supposedly left Bayport—obviously it never got all the way out of town—with a woman and a thirteen-year-old girl in it. They're both blond. We know Danny has stopped at least one car, because he stopped a police car and tried to talk a policewoman, who is a very pretty blond, into giving him her gun. If he stopped this other car—"

"Oh," Gwen said. "Oh, yes, and the location—but how can I help?"

"He held you prisoner. If he had another captive, where might he have put her? We know she wasn't in your apartment—" He came to a complete halt.

"What is it?" Quinn asked, seeing the stricken look on Shigata's face.

"We don't know any such thing. What about that upstairs apartment? He was in it. You said you heard somebody—"

"And he could have held her in it. Yeah." Quinn wiped his face with his right hand. "You're right. He could have.

But all I can say is I never heard a sound from up there, except him walking around, and you know how long I was there."

"Did he keep you gagged?" Shigata asked Gwen.

"No. He did tie me, but he untied me some and let me walk around, go to the bathroom, get a drink of water. Remember, I did escape. Can't you go check the—What's wrong?"

"The building came down," Quinn said. "That's where I got this." He held up the broken wrist. Then he looked at Shigata. "You didn't tell her?"

Shigata shook his head. "How much can one person handle at one time? No. I was going to tell her today."

"That doesn't matter," Gwen said. "Surely you don't think I was going to go back and live there. But about the woman and girl—I got away. She—whoever she was—could have done the same. Why not?"

Shigata was shaking his head.

"She's—very passive." How else can you describe a woman who lived as many years as Melissa had, in the kind of situation her marriage to Sam had been, without making any effort to escape? "She's very passive," he repeated. "She—It's like she doesn't understand she has a right not to be hurt."

"Maybe," Quinn said. "But don't forget she has Gail with her now. And you know what she'll do to protect Gail."

"You know her?" Gwen said, her eyes intent on his face. Then she said, "Your wife? Is it—"

"Not yet," Shigata said. He made a conscious effort to pull himself together. "All right. They may have been in the upstairs apartment. Quinn doesn't think they were there. You think if they were there they would have escaped. If she wasn't there, where—"

"He held me in Dan's condo," Gwen said. "He didn't have anybody else there at that time. But he likes the condo. He likes trashing it. He answered the phone one time. I heard that. Then he called somebody, but I couldn't hear what he said. After that he pulled the phone out and used it to knock a hole in the wall. He—liked having a prisoner there. After I got away, he could have taken somebody else there. I've got the combination."

"I've got it, too," Shigata said. "Thank you. I've got it. I've got it—and a consent to search it."

"I thought we were going by my place," Quinn said.

"We don't have time. Not now."

Shigata entered the combination on the brass touch pad by the door. The door didn't beep at him, and it didn't open.

Of course it didn't. This kind of lock functioned on electricity, and there wasn't any now. He pushed on the door. With an electronic lock, it should have been impossible to open with the power off, but it opened easily. Somebody had done something to the lock.

A stench in some ways worse than that he had encountered in the laundromat greeted him. Behind him, Quinn swore and then said, "I'm sorry, I can't—"

Quinn bolted back down the stairs, and Shigata went on into the condo.

There wasn't one piece of furniture that was both intact and clean. Yellow streams of dried urine decorated the television set. The huge couch was soaked. The room was littered with broken glass, torn-up books, other kinds of debris. Six linen napkins had been unfolded and placed in a neat circle on the floor; each one had been defecated on. In the kitchen, what looked like the entire contents of the refrigerator and all the cupboards lay in a smashed heap on the floor.

A closet door had been demolished. Inside it was a back-pack and an assortment of other gear. "What's that?" asked Quinn.

"I thought you were staying outside."

"I got through puking. Now I'm inside. What's that stuff?"

"Mountain-climbing gear. There's a couple of things missing."

"How do you know?"

"I used to climb some, when I was in college."

"Crazy," Quinn commented.

"You said it. After I broke my collarbone and broke my wrist I figured that out. Quinn, he's taken the rope and the ice ax. What would he want with those?"

"How do you know he took them? How do you know they were here to start with?"

"Dust patterns. They were here. They haven't been gone long. Not over a day or two at the most. What would he—"

"I'm thinking," Quinn said. "Can we get out of here? The air outside's nice and fresh."

"Yeah," Shigata said. But instead of walking out the door, he walked out onto the balcony. Looking into the distance he could still see Melissa's car, wedged in the dike where Bayshore Road curved around it. It had washed there in the flood. The part of the road that was flooded—

The service station.

He didn't know he'd said it aloud until Quinn repeated. "Service station?"

"Yeah," Shigata said. "Service station. If you've got a flat, where do you stop? Service station. And if she couldn't get back out, there's only one place she could go."

"Inside the service station?" Quinn asked. "You mean that Exxon station at Bayshore and I-45? Man, that's seven feet underwater. She couldn't have—"

"She's not stupid," Shigata said. "She knows the area. Where would *you* go?"

"Under the bridge."

"And that's why he took the rope, to climb down there and get her. Come on, we don't know how far ahead of us he is."

Shigata took the stairs two at a time, hearing Quinn panting behind him, and ran for the Bronco. The engine was running by the time Quinn, his face chalky with pain and exhaustion, swung the passenger door open.

Quinn wasn't in too much pain to grab the microphone with his right hand and yell into it, "Car one needs backup at the Bayshore Road on-ramp to I-45. Ten-eighteen, no, make that ten-thirty-nine."

Shigata wasn't too frantic to say, quickly, "Ten-eighteen. Maximum safe speed only."

Quinn repeated that into the radio. Ten-eighteen is flashing lights and sirens and step on it. Ten-thirty-nine is floorboard it.

Running ten-eighteen sometimes causes accidents. Running ten-thirty-nine frequently causes accidents.

Mark Shigata was chief of the whole police department.

There was a man who tied a knot. He could not be conquered as long as the knot was intact. Nobody could untie the knot, until a man came who cut the knot.

I have tied a knot. I do not have to get back up the rope. I am dead; it does not matter if I lie down under the bridge. It is as good a place to lie down as any. As long as the woman lies down with me.

He dropped from the rope onto the ground, untied the ice ax from his belt, and edged cautiously under the bridge.

They were still asleep, the blond woman and the blond girl. He raised the ice ax.

Do I want to do it this way? Do I want them to be asleep? Or do I want to wake them first?

He didn't have the choice. Gail turned over, woke, and screamed.

The Bronco stopped on I-45 at the top of the off-ramp. It wasn't possible to drive all the way down, because Bayshore Road at the foot of the on-ramp was still a river. But how far down could he get? Far enough down to walk to the side of the bridge, rather than climb down on a rope he didn't happen to have?

He reached for the lever to switch into four-wheel drive before beginning, cautiously, to inch as far down as he could go. He had his hand on the lever when he heard the scream.

He couldn't, later, remember switching the ignition off or putting on the emergency brake. Maybe he did those things, or maybe Quinn did, or maybe it was sheer luck the Bronco didn't roll into the river below.

He opened the door, vaulted out, and landed on his side on the sloping ground, catching himself just in time to keep from rolling. It was hard to run on the slope, but he managed.

A zombie. That was all Melissa could think of, looking at the apparition, smelling the filth and decay that came from his clothes and body. A long cut across his abdomen was gaping wide, running with infection. His eyes were glassy.

"What are you doing?" Melissa shouted.

"You have to die," he said, in a very reasonable tone of voice. "I'm already dead. They killed my mother and I killed some of them and now they killed me. I am dead but you have to go with me."

*   *   *

Shigata couldn't fire.

He had his pistol in his hands, but he didn't dare fire it because if he missed he would hit Melissa or Gail. If he didn't miss, if he hit Danny, Danny would fall forward, and his ax, from the position he was standing in now, would fall into Melissa's skull.

Shigata began to edge around so that he could hit Danny from a position that would make Danny fall backward instead of forward. Then he realized that from where he was, that was impossible. He would have to go around to the other side of the bridge, go down the on-ramp, to get at the right angle.

But that wouldn't be the right angle either, because Melissa and Gail would be in his line of fire.

And there wasn't enough time for that.

Trying to move completely soundlessly, he continued to edge toward Danny—but he couldn't move soundlessly. The ground was completely waterlogged. Grass slid under his feet. Twice, three times, he nearly fell into the foaming water below.

He was close enough now to hear Gail screaming. "Go away. Go away now!"

Melissa wasn't saying anything. Then she did. "Gail, try to get up on top of the bridge. You can get help that way."

"Mommy!"

"Go on! Go get help!"

Shigata could see Gail backing away, turning, climbing toward the off-ramp. She was safe—nobody was at risk now but Melissa. Melissa, whom he loved more than he loved life. More than he loved anybody or anything he'd ever known in his life.

He was close enough to see her, close enough to hear her, but not close enough to save her.

She would fight for Gail, he knew that. But Gail was safe

now. Never in her life had Melissa been willing to fight for herself.

He continued to edge closer. For the first time he heard Danny's voice.

"You let her get away." There was a distinct whine.

"You have to go now," Melissa said. Her tone was completely reasonable.

"I'm dead. I have to lie down."

"That's right," she said, "you are dead. I can tell it. So go away."

"You have to lie down with me."

"No, I don't. I was dead but I'm not anymore. I quit being dead."

"Women are wanton. You will lie down with any man."

"Not any more I won't. Only with one man."

"With me."

"No. Not with you. Go away. Go away, or I'll kill you."

"You can't kill me. I'm dead. I'm already dead."

"If you're dead then go to your grave."

"I have to take you with me."

Shigata was almost in position. He raised his pistol, aimed more carefully than he had ever aimed before in his life, and squeezed the trigger.

And heard another shot, at almost exactly the same second as his own. He lowered the pistol to see Danny toppling as if in slow motion into the water below.

To see Melissa, the pistol he'd given her still in her hand, lowering her arm slowly as she turned to see where the other shot had come from.

To see Melissa dropping the gun and staring at him, to see Gail coming back under the bridge screaming "Mommy!" and stopping, too, to stare open-mouthed at the body caught in the flood, turning to stare at Shigata.

He must've holstered his pistol, because it wasn't in his

hand any longer, and surely he would have better sense than to drop it on the muddy ground.

He heard sirens—the backups he'd asked for, arriving too late.

Shigata made his way toward them, walking at first but almost running despite the slope as he got nearer. Catching them both at once in an enormous bear hug, he felt himself sobbing with relief.

They were both hugging him. Both of them. Melissa as well as Gail. Then he forgot Danny, forgot police cars and police officers, forgot everything but Melissa in his arms. The floodgates of six months of repression surged open, and his mouth went down hard on hers.

Then he pulled back for a moment. But only a moment. "Gail, go to the car," he said.

"Which car? The Bronco?"

"Yes. The Bronco. There are some sandwiches in there. Go get one and sit in the back seat and eat it."

He felt, rather than saw, Gail head toward the car. He had both arms around Melissa now, and his face was pressed down against hers. His hips were pushing hers and his whole body was trembling.

Then he remembered. Remembered she didn't want him. She'd made that perfectly clear. Remembered she was a grown woman and had the right to make her own decisions and finally, finally, she was willing to fight for herself.

She didn't belong to him. He stopped.

He turned her loose and walked a few steps away from her, facing away from her, one hand on a concrete pylon, breathing. Just breathing.

Melissa, walking after him, walking around him to look at his face, saw his black eyes gazing into an unimaginable distance. He had gone far away from her. She didn't know where he had gone.

Wherever it was it must not be a happy place, because tears were coursing down his face.

"Why, Mark?" she asked.

"Why what?" he answered, turning to look at her.

"Why did you stop?"

"You know why I stopped." He turned away again.

"No, I don't. I don't know. You were kissing me and you stopped and I don't know why you stopped. Mark—"

"What do you want, Melissa? In six months you've never once, never for one second, let me know what you *want.* In the name of Almighty God, will you please tell me what you *want?*"

"I want you to kiss me some more."

It was the first thing she'd ever asked him for, and he spun unbelievingly to look at her, at the brilliant blue eyes, at the silver-fair hair he wouldn't believe was real except that he knew it was, at the delicate, child-woman face. Then he took her in his arms again and this time he didn't stop.

This might be the only time I ever hold her. The only time. I will take everything she will give me, now, everything I can decently take in the daylight.

Deliberately he let himself feel it. Feel all of it. He opened his mind and body to the pleasure and let the pleasure build.

The sweetness of her mouth was overwhelming, and he was fully conscious of her hips at the level of his, of her arms around him, and of the pleasure that went on building until quite suddenly, involuntarily, unexpectedly, it exploded and his groan was stifled by her mouth on his.

He didn't ask if she knew what had happened. He knew she knew. Perhaps he should be ashamed, perhaps he should be embarrassed, but all he felt was an odd triumph he couldn't begin to understand.

He went on holding her, feeling the pounding of his

heart gradually slowing to normal as every nerve and muscle in his body began to relax.

Then he kissed her, once, lightly, and stepped back a little again. He tried to let go of her hand but she wouldn't let him.

That is the second thing she has ever asked me for.

So he went on holding her hand for a moment and then, again, enclosed her in his arms. They stood in complete silence until Quinn stopped somewhere behind Shigata and said, "I've got the ME's investigator en route."

"Uh huh," Shigata said, and reluctantly backed away from Melissa and tried, again, to let go of her hand.

And once again she wouldn't let him.

Quinn turned and walked back toward the Bronco. The pain in his wrist was blue, and he was sick with it, but this moment was worth everything. He'd ordered Barndt—she was the only other officer on the scene—to stay at the top of the hill and keep everybody else back. He was glad he had.

"You've got to let go of me or marry me," Shigata said.

"When?" Melissa asked immediately.

"When what?"

Melissa shook her head and dropped his hand. This time it was she who turned away. "I don't want to play," she said over her shoulder.

"I understand," he said, feeling like a lead weight was dropping down on his chest, crushing out of him the life that only moments ago had surged through him.

"No, you don't understand. You try and try and try to understand me and you never just *ask.*"

"All right, I'm asking. What is it you want me to understand?"

"Mark, can you make me feel like—like that? Like you—"

"You've never—?"

"No," she said, the word half a sob. "When would I have? With Sam? You know what he did to me. With the—the—paying customers?"

"Melissa, please forget that. Please, please, please, let yourself—"

"Can you make me forget it? Mark, can you? Can anybody? Ever?"

"I don't know," he said. "Melissa, I don't know. I can sure as hell try. But I think—I think you've got to decide to forget it. I love you. That's all I know. And when you love someone you don't want that person hurt."

"I didn't want to feel. They hurt me. Everybody hurt me. Everybody always—"

"I know, Melissa. Truly, I know."

"But you didn't hurt me. I started to feel again and that scared me. Mark, I've been so scared so long—"

"Did I scare you? I didn't mean to—"

"No. You didn't scare me. And that was what scared me. Mark—when—when will you—"

This time he did understand and didn't pretend not to. He avoided looking at her as he answered. "I—have a moral code, Melissa," he said. "You can call it a cockeyed one if you want to. I didn't mean what just happened to happen. I really didn't. And—and—I won't take you to bed without marrying you. I'm sorry, Melissa. I won't. I can't. If I didn't love you, it wouldn't matter and maybe I would, but I do love you, and it does matter, and I won't. I'm sorry."

"Don't be sorry."

"Why?"

"That's the nicest thing anybody has ever said to me."

Now he did look at her—looked at her and walked toward her to catch her in his arms again—and when he finally backed off it was Melissa who was breathing hard.

"Mark?"

"Yes?"

"Is the courthouse open today?"

"I don't know."

"Can you find out?"

"Yes. I'll find out. I'll find out, Melissa. But right now I've got some work to do. I wish I didn't. But I do."

With his arm around her waist, he turned to greet Joel Moran.

They walked down the stairs of the courthouse together, Mark and Melissa, Al Quinn and Nguyen, with Gail deliberately splashing in every puddle of muddy water she could find. It didn't matter. Nobody had gone home to change clothes.

"Gail?" Nguyen said.

Gail scampered back. Nguyen was one of her favorite people.

"I think the baby is getting a little bit of a rash and I'm ver', ver' tired. I got those extra boys till their daddy come get them. And Al got hurt. I need help. Can you come spend the night and help me out?"

"My mom and dad just got married," Gail said doubtfully. "I don't know if—"

"I know it's a lot to ask," Nguyen said, "but really—"

"Well—" Gail looked at Shigata.

"I guess it's okay this time."

Shigata lay on his back, eyes open, staring at the darkened ceiling. Melissa was still crying, her head on his left shoulder, his left arm curved around her back. She'd said a lot, but the only thing that had been coherent was what she was still saying over and over. "I didn't know. I didn't know. I didn't know."

He didn't know what to say, so he didn't say anything, and she kept crying. Finally he answered, "Thank God I was the one to teach you."

"Yes," she said. The sobs died away and she lay with her head on his shoulder, not crying now. "I'm sorry I cried."

"Don't be. You needed to."

The telephone rang.

"Oh, hell," Shigata said.

"Telephone's back on."

"Yeah. I noticed."

The telephone went on ringing, and Shigata got out of bed and walked across the room to answer it. "Yeah," he said. "Yeah. All right. On the way."

The lights came on quite suddenly.

Shigata hung up the phone and grabbed for clean—but slightly damp—underwear. As he had feared, the whole house was damp from water that had forced its way in, even through the walls.

He got a clean, if slightly damp, pair of wash-and-wear pants out of the closet and pulled them on. He wasn't in the FBI anymore. He didn't have to wear suits and starched shirts all of the time.

"Sorry," he said, sitting down on the bed to put on socks and shoes.

"I guess that's what happens when you marry a cop," Melissa said. "He has to get up and go places at all the wrong times."

He grinned at her, letting his eyes rest on her naked body and making sure she knew he was looking.

"Yep. That's what happens when you marry a cop." He pulled on a sweatshirt and reached for his gun belt.

"It sure it. I'll be back in a couple of hours. I'll be back, Melissa. I'll always be back."

ANNE WINGATE is a former police officer, the veteran of eight years of police work in Georgia and Texas, where she was a qualified latent-fingerprint expert. She now lives in Salt Lake City, Utah.